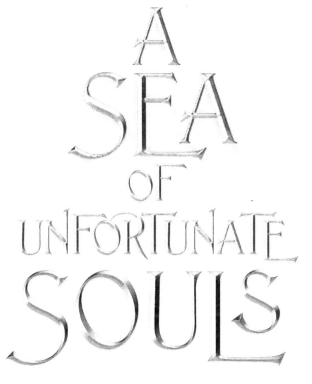

DARK AND TWISTED TALES

Book One

Copyright © 2022 by Jay R. Wolf

First Edition: All Rights Reserved.

No part of this book may be reproduced in any form or by any electronic or mechanical means, including information storage and retrieval systems, without written permission from the author, except for the use of brief quotations in a book review. This book is a work of fiction. Names, characters places and incidents either are the product of the authors' imagination or are used fictitiously. Any resemblance to actual events, locales, or persons, living or dead is purely coincidental.

ISBN 978-1-7351315-6-6 (eBook)

ISBN 978-1-7351315-7-3 (paperback)

Published by Night Muse Press

Cover Art by Maria Spada

Character Art by Kalynne Art

Book Art by Nathan Hansen illustrations

Editing by Clare Sager

Proofreading by Fantasy Proofs

Formatted by R. L. Davennor

NIGHT MUSE PRESS
EST. 2020

CONTENT WARNING

This novel contains graphic depictions of violence and death and adult language. It is intended for a mature adult audience.

The seas are full of dangers, so continue at your own risk...

To my grandmother, who always knew I'd do great things.

Mugga,

This one is for you.

1. ULTIMATUM

I HAD TO GET THE *HELLS* OUT OF HERE.

Silver shackles dug into my ankles, clinking as I moved. I pressed my head against the cool stone wall and cursed at the pain. The sting was nothing compared to the burn of the iron bars next to me. Iron and sea witches didn't get along, and the fact that my captor knew this made escaping nearly impossible.

Every part of my soul wished to be back on the *Black Betty*, surrounded by the crew who'd become family. Instead, I was held in a cage like some animal. Nearly a decade of being at sea and not once had I been imprisoned, yet here I sat awaiting judgment. Guess that's what happens when you thwart the plans of a king.

Ignoring the smell of piss and shit, I stood and paced the cell. It was small, just three walls and the bars to keep me company. Well, that and the critters that frequented the prisons of Khan. After a few paces, the agony of pain in my leg had faded to a dull throb. My boots scuffed across the stone floor as I hatched an escape plan, working out every detail over and over in my head until it was engraved into my memory.

My ears buzzed with silence until a rat skidded across the floor, stopping to collect the few crumbs from my dinner plate before scurrying off again.

I shivered, and wished Keenan were with me. I missed the deep throated laugh that lit his face up. If he were here maybe the nightmares would be more bearable. He was the only one on my crew who knew what had happened all those years ago. I owed him everything and now he, and the rest of my crew, were locked up somewhere in this prison. I clenched my jaw.

Now that King Roland had me in his grasp, he'd never let me go. Either he'd keep me here in this cell or execute me. I just wished he'd get on with it.

Three days of being away from the sea and my ship. Every inch of me wanted to scream with rage. The idea of never sailing again, of never tasting the salt on my tongue or feeling the euphoria of water on my skin sent my stomach twisting into knots.

No. I couldn't let that happen. The sea was my life, and I was its living, breathing soul. There wasn't another who connected with her spirit as I did. Some found it odd to think of the sea as a tangible living being, but she was. She called to me, spoke to me when I needed guidance. Once, she almost killed me in her icy, airless clutches. Somehow I'd managed to survive and every day since, I'd belonged to her. As a child, I'd feared the sea and refused to go anywhere near it, but now she was my home, and I would find my way back no matter the cost.

Distant murmurs cut through the silence. I froze, then moved closer to the bars, hissing at the burn against my skin. Three guards. All of them sported red and black waistcoats, though only one had a golden medallion sewn on its front. The mark of a kingsman—a servant to King Roland himself. I wanted nothing more than to rip it from his shirt and shove it down his throat. The other two were just prison guards; one held a cigar between his lips while the other bounced on the heels of his boots.

"I heard she has the head of every monster she's ever killed hanging from the walls in her quarters," the man with the cigar said.

"Is it true she boarded Captain Hook's ship and stole half his treasure from right under his nose?"

I bit my tongue to keep from laughing. Both claims were true. I wondered who'd spread the truth. My crew enjoyed telling tales of their captain's endeavors. Those, however, were usually exaggerated and meant to deter other pirates.

The rumor about Hook was my favorite one of all the rumors. The captain and I hadn't exactly been friendly, and the last time we saw one another was during a hunt. I'd been searching the seas for a serpent that was terrorizing the coast of Darenshire. It just so happened that Hook was doing the same. Both of us ended up bruised and bloodied and it wasn't from the serpent. The look on his face when we parted was one I'd never forget.

"You're both morons. Pipe down and let's get this show on the road. The last thing I need is another scolding from his royal pain in my—"

"I sincerely hope you aren't speaking about our beloved king." A figure slipped from the shadows, his voice alone sending rage coursing through every vein in my body. A black hood covered his face, but that didn't fool me. I'd know that voice anywhere. The wizard.

"I—I..." The kingsman stepped back and waved his hands as if that would do much good against magic.

"*Tsk tsk*, Siebold. Where is she?" He cackled, sending shivers down my back.

I swore under my breath and scurried from the bars, grateful to be away from the thing causing me pain even if I was about to be subjected to a much worse fate. I'd have happily let the iron kill me if it weren't for the fact that my men were held up somewhere in this prison, too.

They were all I had in this god-forsaken life... and *Black Betty*, of course.

Laggard footsteps echoed in the hall. Dread replaced my anger as a flicker of light came into view followed by a hood. The wizard curled his hands around the iron bars without worry of being burned.

Show off.

"Ah, if it isn't Arie the Monster Hunter. Or do you go by sea witch?" His exaggerated sweeping bow had me rolling my eyes.

"Piss off," I snarled, wishing more than ever that Slayer was by my side. Maybe then I wouldn't feel so naked in front of an enemy.

He laughed again, lowering his hood to reveal light, unkempt hair. Small scars crisscrossed along a pale face, and his right eye had clouded over completely, the other a deep brown. One of the scars, larger and more grotesque than the others, stretched from his brow to cross at his nose, ending at the bottom of his chin.

My skin crawled. I'd first met him on a bounty; he'd been torturing a man who knew the whereabouts of the monster I hunted. It was the first time I'd seen madness in someone's eyes.

"Your tongue is as vile as I would expect from a pirate. I do hope the king allows me to play with you when he's through. Do you like to play games?"

I'd very much like to slice my blade through your throat and watch you bleed. Instead, I bit out, "What do you want?"

"I've come to deliver a message. An ultimatum if you will."

As a monster hunter, I'd accepted my death a long time ago. I always imagined it would be at the hands of one of the beasts I chased, certainly not a tyrant like King Roland. "You can tell the king to piss off."

The wizard's grin widened until I could see his gums. "I like you." He paused and shrugged. "I suppose you *don't* want your freedom then."

There was no way the king would allow such a thing, not even if I begged. He had been trying to catch me for months after I may or may not have set fire to a small fleet under his protection. It wasn't *my* fault that they just happened to be in the way of a bounty I had come to collect. Still, the thought of making it out in one piece piqued my interest. "You mentioned an ultimatum. That means I either assist him, or I die, and I would gladly choose death over helping him."

The wizard leaned in, pressing his face between the bars until his nose poked through, a smug grin on his face. Why did he look so pleased?

"Oh, he doesn't plan on killing *you*, little dove."

I dug my nails into my palms. Would the king stoop to killing my crew? I huffed, of course he would, recalling the time he'd burned down an entire village simply because they weren't producing crops to his satisfaction. I wasn't going to let this mad man scare me. I'd have to find a way out before anyone died. "I still won't agree to whatever it is he wants me to do."

A laugh echoed through the empty hall. "Oh, this is going to be fun."

He threw up his hands, and a bright light shot from his palms. I stumbled backward, falling hard on the floor. Pain shot up my arm, and my eyes burned. I tried to shield them from the light, but it was little use. It pierced every tiny gap, searing into my skull in pure white-hot agony. I screamed and gasped for breath as my eyes fluttered before succumbing to the darkness.

Loud chatter pulled me from unconsciousness. Blood pounded in my head as I tried to focus on the sound, but my ringing ears made that difficult. Where was I? Slowly, I opened my eyes and blinked away the blur. Dozens of faces were fixated on me. Men and women sat in rows along the circular room. Some whispered while they stared and I could only imagine what they thought.

I forced my gaze elsewhere and instead found I was strapped to a wooden chair. I shifted and waves of pins and needles shot up both arms. I bit my tongue to keep from crying out and blinked away tears. My wrists burned with a vengeance, the skin beneath the shackles hissing and cracking in a way that made my stomach turn.

These weren't the same shackles. These were made with iron. I swallowed bile and forced my attention back to my surroundings.

At what I presumed to be the front, King Roland spoke in hushed tones with a guard. He sat on a throne carved of glass, or perhaps crystal. It reflected the lights that dangled above, casting a rainbow of colors along the walls.

This was the first time I'd ever been this up close and personal with the king of Khan. He was nothing more than an overweight tyrant balder than a newborn baby. He wore an oversized surcoat embellished in red and black embroidery. On his chest was the same medallion as Siebold: a dragon curled around an ornate sword decorated in rubies.

King Roland paled into insignificance against the contraption behind him. Raised on a large platform stood Guilly, dried blood coated its blade making me grimace. King Roland was known for his ruthless measures when it came to death, and nothing was more famous than his guillotine. Rumor was he named it after killing Gillian—an even more notorious pirate than myself. He'd brought him to the town square and beheaded him. Afterward he'd had the head embalmed and placed at the docks for all to see.

How many people had he killed with it? I suppose there were worse ways to die—at least it would be quick.

King Roland lifted a hand. As the murmurs died down, he cleared his throat. "Good evening, fellow members of the court. I've summoned you here today to bear witness to the sentencing of one Arie Lockwood. Pirate, monster hunter, and sea witch. There will be no trial today. There is no need, not when we all know this one is guilty of treason to the throne."

Guilt presumed that I had done something wrong, when really, it was he who should be sitting here. My transgressions were nothing compared to a king who raided towns and pillaged farmlands. Hundreds of people in Khan lived in poverty while this man sat on a throne of cut crystal in a gilded palace. He was the monster, and I was a monster *hunter*.

The crowd erupted in a chorus of boos until the king raised his hand. "But I believe there is something else that can be done about Ms. Lockwood."

I snarled. "I already told your wizard. I won't help you, so you might as well kill me and get this over with."

Gasps cut through the crowd as all eyes focused on King Roland. The sea of pale faces and startled looks said all I needed to know—they feared this man. A king who had taken a beautiful place like Khan and defiled it with his need for power and greed. The lands were wilting away and yet he only cared about himself.

I refused to bow to a man who hid behind his title and terrorized his people, leaving them with scraps, or nothing at all.

Stacia, a little girl I'd come to know during my travels, had come running down to the docks where we'd been getting ready to set sail. Her tear ridden face still haunted my dreams. I didn't have to go far before I saw what bothered her. Her family's barn was on fire surrounded by Roland's men. They hooted and hollered as the screams inside grew louder and more terrifying. When I asked Stacia what had happened, all she could muster was that King Roland was mad her daddy couldn't afford the new tax increase. So rather than steal his land, or his belongings, the king burned down the barn with him and his wife inside.

In one sweep she'd lost both of her parents, something I related to very well. Thankfully, she had an aunt who lived a few towns away and was happy to know her niece was okay. I'd left her with the same advice once given to me upon my parents death: past sorrows make for brighter tomorrows. It wasn't much, but it was enough. There were whispers that Stacia had left years later for the Enchanted Realm to join some sort of guild, but as far as I knew, she'd been doing okay.

I sucked in a deep breath, failing to put out the rage that burned within. I'd have given anything to show him the wrath of Slayer if we were in different circumstances. I tugged on my restraints and bit my cheek to keep from crying out from the pain. Copper laced my tongue as I narrowed my eyes on the king. What I wouldn't give to release my gift and bring the wrath of it down upon him.

The king stood from his throne, descending a few steps until he towered over me. Icy blue eyes scrutinized me as if he were trying to force me to do as he pleased with his will. I met his gaze, allowing him to see just how much I loathed him.

He lowered himself until his breath touched my ear, the stink nearly making me gag. "You have no say here, hunter, and what I need from you is something I think is in your best interest to consider."

I huffed. "Why would I do that?"

"We'll get to that, but first…" He turned toward the crowd. "One week ago, I sent men to search Scarlett's Lagoon for our missing fleet. The fleet had been in search of some stolen cargo."

A gasp escaped before I could stop it. Scarlett's Lagoon? What were they thinking? Anyone with a brain knew to steer clear of the Leviathan's lair. I might have been an expert when it came to hunting the evil that dwelled in the sea, but even I knew better than to sail to my death.

"They have gone missing, and I'm sure you all know why." He looked at me then. "You can sail to Scarlett's Lagoon, kill the beast and bring back what was lost or watch those you love die before your very eyes."

My entire body froze, breath catching in my throat. This lunatic wanted to send me to face the deadliest monster in the sea and would kill every last man on my crew if I didn't. The mere notion of never besting Nathaniel at cards, or watching Hector and Keenan flaunt over who was strongest, was a life I didn't want to know. None of this made any sense. What did he have to gain? After all, there was a saying when it came to the Leviathan: *Just don't.*

It was simple, really. Leave the big, angry, man-eating beast alone, and you live. Threaten him and you're *going* to meet your maker.

Only a few had ever lived to tell the tale of the Leviathan, and the only one who did so without becoming a mindless lunatic was Captain Hook.

I wasn't about to be its next meal. I may be a monster hunter, but that didn't mean I wanted to go after that thing. "You're out of your fu—"

Something zapped me, sending my entire body into a convulsing fit. Agonizing pain rippled along my skin, the iron dug deeper and I cried out. I sucked in sharp breaths and concentrated on not passing out. I coughed, my throat dry and limbs weak as the pain slowly subsided. I'd never felt something so painful before and when I turned to see what had happened, the wizard came into focus.

"*Tsk tsk*, little dove, mind your tongue in front of our king." He smirked, hands at his back as he skipped, literally skipped like a little girl, to stand next to his king. "Continue, Your Majesty."

King Roland cleared his throat. "It appears the monster hunter needs some convincing." He nodded toward a guard who left through a side door.

While everyone waited in silence, I considered a new escape plan. I just needed some way to get these iron cuffs off my wrists. There were only three guards who stood by King Roland. I didn't have Slayer, but if I got my hands on one of their swords, maybe I'd stand a chance.

Just as I worked out a plan, the door flung open and a guard strode in. A slight woman with a sack over her head thrashed against his hold. I narrowed my eyes; why the hells would this girl's life matter to me when they had my men locked up?

"It took us a long time to figure out the best leverage against you. Your men are loyal to you, as you are to them. Using them is not only foolish, but unproductive. After all, you will need your crew." He paused then, leaning to look into my eyes. "I have to ask… how did you get them to do that? To be willing to die for you."

I opened my mouth to give a snarky retort, but he waved a hand.

"I decided to dig harder, deeper. It appears that you weren't always a monster hunter. You lived in a small village with your parents. *Male* parents." He spat.

I stiffened. How the hells did he know that? I'd left that life behind, hidden those parts as deep as I could. Hadn't I? My eyes widened, if someone told him about them then that meant—

"Blasphemy, two men sharing a bed, it's a good thing they got what they deserved. But that wasn't the only thing we found."

No. My throat tightened, heart pounding as my gaze shifted to the woman who was now sitting on the floor with a blade at her neck. He didn't mean—

"You have a sister."

I couldn't think. Couldn't breathe. Bile built up and I swallowed, not wanting to show weakness in front of the king but it did no good. My entire world was about to collide with another—one I had worked so hard to never let out. My heart hammered in my chest.

It couldn't be.

A smirk rose on the king's lips as he slid back into the seat of his throne, satisfaction written all over his face. He was so sure he'd won.

And hadn't he? I knew exactly who lay on the floor in front of me. The real question was, how did he? No one was supposed to know about her. I'd paid a lot of gold to keep her a secret.

"Take off that ridiculous sack," the king demanded.

A guard stepped forward and obeyed, sending a wave of blonde curls in every direction. A single streak of blue hair hung over her face. The girl looked up, the terrified look in her green eyes sending daggers into my heart.

Frankie.

From her single dimple to the too-large-for-that-head ears, she looked so familiar and yet at the same time so different. My fathers had died a few days before her tenth birthday; it was hard to imagine that we'd been apart for that long.

Tears strolled down from red and swollen eyes, one of them sporting a bruise and I lurched forward, forgetting I was strapped to a chair. The iron dug deeper, and I cried out as something wet slid down my hand. I was bleeding, but she… someone had hurt her.

"Who did that?" I snarled. Anger crashed over me like a tsunami, begging me to unleash my magic but the iron cuffs stopped that with a zap to my wrists. I coughed through the pain, bringing my gaze back to the man who towered over Frankie.

"She bites." The guard who brought her out rubbed his reddening hand, had Frankie actually bitten him? I stifled my laugh and instead memorized the hooked curve of this guard's nose, and the darkened eyes that refused to look anywhere else besides Frankie. I'd never forget his face, and one day he would be a dead man.

"Arie?" her voice cracked, her lips chapped and bleeding. How long had they kept her captive?

"Hey kid, you okay?"

"Ah, good," Pascal interrupted. "We did get the right girl."

King Roland leaned forward, his voice low. "You can save her and leave with both of your lives. But before you do, you will take down the Leviathan and bring back what is mine. If you don't, well, I think you can guess what will be done." He nodded toward Guilly.

"Why me? Why not send your wizard?"

He sat back. "While he may be good against human enemies, he doesn't have the ability or knowledge you do when it comes to taking down sea monsters. He will, however, be tagging along on your mission."

The hells he would. Having that man on my ship would cause more than just unease with my men. I bit my tongue from protesting. I needed to keep my cool if I was going to get everyone out of this alive.

"I need to make sure that you aren't going to just turn around and try to break your sister out. You can't be too careful when dealing with a witch." King Roland paused. "So, tell me, Hunter, are you prepared to accept?"

The answer was clear, and he knew it. There was nothing I could do but fight for her life. To sail into the gates of hell and hope to the sea gods I came out alive. Without hesitation, I nodded.

For my sister, I would do anything.

11. EYE OF THE STORM

"TEN MINUTES. SAY YOUR GOODBYES." The guard shoved me into the cell and locked it before arms wrapped around my middle, suffocating me. I didn't want to let go, let alone speak. My sister was *here*. This was worse than any nightmare I'd ever had.

"Are you okay?" My voice cracked as I blinked away tears. I pressed my chin to her head, inhaling the smell of honey and sage. She may have grown into a young woman, but some things never changed. Frankie wasn't my sister by blood, but we were loved by the same fathers: Malakai and Viktor. After their deaths, I hadn't wanted to leave her behind, and she fought me every step of the way, but it was a necessity. I couldn't let what happened stand, but I knew leaving her with people who'd care for her was the best option. I'd promised I would return, and I'd always planned to find her once all this was over.

It took much longer than I'd expected, and now here she was.

Frankie released me abruptly and stepped back with narrowed eyes. "That was because it's good to see you. But this is for what you did."

"What?" I didn't have a chance to react before she hit me square in the jaw. I stumbled back, nearly losing my footing before she was on me, fists pummeling me in rapid succession. I blocked her right hook but missed the knee to my gut and toppled over, coughing as pain tore through my abdomen. I sucked in deep breaths as she backed away. She paced along the bars; hands balled into fists at her side.

"What the *fuck* was that for?" I hissed.

Where had Frankie learned how to fight like that? When had she become *this*? I wished we had more time together so I could find out. I wanted to know everything that had happened to her down to the very last detail. Eight years apart seemed much longer than it was. For her, hating me was more pressing than wanting to know about what I'd done during that time away. I had become an entirely different person—apparently, so had she. Hells, I'd overcome my fears to travel the waters in search of our fathers' killer. She had to understand, to know that I was doing all of this for us.

That night when everything changed, I'd walked into our house to find my fathers dead and her cowering under my bed clutching a knife. She was shaking and scared, and we sat on that floor, crying together for hours. She'd fallen asleep in my arms. Hearing her faint cries had been the catalyst for what I had to do next. I swore to find the one responsible and not stop until I did. A few days later, I set a course for the seas and left her with friends of Malakai and Viktor who'd promised to take care of her. Seeing her now, I wondered if I'd done the right thing.

"Let's see, leaving me alone with the Andersons for starters. The fact that you didn't come back to get me like you promised you would. Getting me kidnapped."

Every word she uttered was like another blow to my stomach. I *had* done those things, though at the time I didn't have a choice. What kind of sister would I be if I had brought her onto a ship with pirates to go chase down our fathers' killer? I promised myself I wouldn't return… that I *couldn't* return until the one responsible was found. Having to face her, knowing I'd failed… "The first was to protect you, and I had every intention of coming back for you. As for the third, no one was supposed to know who you were. That was the deal."

She laughed, and for a brief moment I saw the light in her eye, that same look she had as a child. It quickly dissipated leaving behind a hardened shell. I cursed under my breath. An overwhelming desire to kill whoever had harmed her surged through me.

I stilled. It was me.

I was the one who had hurt her, who was the reason she was stuck behind bars.

Curse the gods, what had I done?

"You simply saw me as a burden and gave me away so you could do as you pleased without having the weight of your sister on your conscience. Did you even think about me while you were parading around as a pirate queen?"

How could she actually think, let alone believe that I would ever leave her behind unless I didn't have a choice? That I didn't think about her every day?

I sucked in a deep breath, exhaling through gritted teeth. "Of *course* I care. Why do you think I didn't want you to come along, Frankie? Once I became a hunter, it became much too dangerous for you to join me. It was the only way to afford my mission. I didn't ask for this life and I sure as hells didn't plan on being gone for so long. I just wanted to protect you."

But was it enough? By giving her the life I never had, I'd hoped it would keep her out of the darkness and headed toward the light. Frankie had always been the brightness in my life. As kids, everyone in town knew her name. When she wasn't befriending some random traveler, she was helping shopkeepers in the market or assisting ships at the docks. There was no doubt in my mind that Frankie would grow up to be something truly amazing.

When I looked at her now, I saw none of that. I only saw the darkness I had worked so hard to stifle.

"I waited for you every day down by the docks, but you never came." Frankie's voice rose as she shot me a glare. "My new family was tired of watching my disappointment, so they packed us up and moved away from the sea. I was so upset that I ran away hoping you would keep your promise and take me away. After a while I realized that you were never coming back. I decided to take matters into my own hands and search for you."

My eyes widened, my jaw nearly reaching the floor. "You idiot, no wonder they found you."

"They found me because *you* were too busy sailing the seas and becoming a hunter to care about me."

"Frankie, I—"

"Why are you even here?" Frankie crossed her arms and turned her back. The hardened shell closed even further. I wasn't getting anything out of her now.

King Roland had only granted us a few minutes to speak, and I didn't want to waste it arguing. I hadn't expected him to approve such a request, but then again, I hadn't expected him to force me to sail toward my death, either. Now wasn't the time to worry about the king's antics.

I had to get her out. Which meant I had no choice but to do what the king demanded.

"You can be mad at me, you can hate me and tell me to drown in the sea, but you are still my sister. Never forget that." I slammed on the bars of our cell, calling for the guard who was standing close enough to listen in. Just because the king had given us a chance to speak, didn't mean he'd do so without a watchful eye.

Frankie snorted.

Another blow, this one hit deeper than all the rest. She really thought I wouldn't come back. Then again, I had never given her a reason to think otherwise. There was nothing I could do about our broken relationship at that moment. It was time to find my men and get back to my ship.

We had a monster to hunt.

It was said to find true happiness, you need to love or be loved. My love happened to be the sea. Now I was back on the *Betty*, my world righted itself, save for the wizard who lurked below deck… much to my dismay. Being caged and away, even for three days, I had wondered if I'd ever return, yet upon my arrival the sea had welcomed me back with open arms, leaving the skies clear and the water calm ever since. Each breath I took was a reminder that I'd never take this for granted. The soft hum of her song drifted around me like a current, dragging me under her spell as it settled inside me.

I missed you too.

King Roland gave us until the next full moon to bring down the Leviathan, which meant we only had a few weeks to get the job done. We'd already been sailing for a few days; Scarlett's Lagoon wasn't necessarily far from the kingdom of Khan, but enough that it left my crew on edge. Having the wizard lurking about didn't help with their unease either. Thanks to Keenan, no one had tried to kill him… yet.

The crew aired their annoyances about our newest guest, but there wasn't much I could do about it. The king made it abundantly clear that he was to tag alone to ensure our success, and if he didn't make it out of this alive, then neither would my crew.

With hope, we'd have plenty of time to get the job done and get back before anything happened to Frankie… or the wizard. For now, I pushed the thought aside and placed my attention on the fine vessel before me.

The *Betty* was built by a Naval captain who'd lost her in a game of cards. Foolish for a captain to bet their ship, especially against me, but I wasn't complaining. Tall, sturdy masts, and black as night, she was all mine.

Men bustled around the ship as if they hadn't been in cages just days ago. I admired their will to keep fighting, to push on no matter what. I'd been their captain for a few years, some had been with me before that, but the moment they stepped foot on this boat, they were my responsibility. They were mine to look after and I wasn't about to fail them now.

Inhaling, I let my lungs fill with the cool air. I closed my eyes and lifted my face to the gathering clouds. Dark and growing with the oncoming storm, I rejoiced in them. In the fact that I could see them again. In the distance, a flash of lightning lit the sky, sending a smile to my face. A storm at sea was its own adventure and with my magic, it made it that much more exhilarating. Controlling the sea and storm had been the first thing I learned to do with my gift.

I didn't know much about how the magic that coursed through my veins worked. I didn't have a teacher, or anyone to explain to me what it all meant. That night, before finding my fathers dead, I'd finally dug up all the courage I had and stepped into the sea. The same one they'd forbidden me from going into. I couldn't resist the call anymore, the voice that had lured me in was as sweet as honey. The battle between fear and need raged inside me. Though something about the song calmed me, pulling me closer and closer with each step I took. When my feet hit the water, my racing heart slowed as life poured into my soul. Everything made sense for the first time in my life.

Wrapping my hands tighter around the wheel, I sighed. Usually, I'd have left the sailing to Mason, my sailing master, but he hadn't survived King Roland's attack. Sorrow crept its way into every crevice and I swallowed a sob. He was the only one who'd died that day and it left most of us shattered. When this was all over, I'd make sure he was given a proper send off.

Giles, our new sailing master, had taken his place but it took a toll on him. He'd been crying when I came out of my quarters this morning, so I sent him to help Keenan. As much as it pained me to stand at the helm, this was where I needed to be. If I was going to die today, I wanted to do it behind the wheel of my most precious ally.

I looked back to the men that, to my surprise, were all in chipper spirits despite what had happened. I had told them our mission, and they knew the dangers. Maybe monsters didn't scare them anymore. The rumors of gold and jewels were said to lurk in the Leviathan's den probably helped matters. Just as well, because I wouldn't want any other crew by my side. They were family.

Guilt tugged at my heart. Frankie was family, and she was stuck behind bars. The longer this mission lasted, the more I worried about what the king would do to her. My mind drifted toward Guilly and its death blade and I shook my head.

I wouldn't let it come to that. We'd sail to the beast's lair, finish it off, and I'd get my sister out before any harm could come to her.

"You all right, Cap?" Keenan, my first mate, stood beside me. His gaze remained fixed on the men below us while he tucked his hands in the pockets of his breeches. His dark shaggy hair was pinned back revealing a set of milky-brown eyes.

"If you ask me that one more time, Kay, I'm going to throw you from the plank and leave you to the monsters."

He laughed. "Threatening your best chance at staying alive now, are we?"

Damn if he wasn't right. I'd lost count a long time ago how many times the man had saved my life. I couldn't help it—there was just something so exhilarating about flirting with death. Even if it meant my men had to save my ass every now and again.

I shook my head, laughter tugging at my lips. "We'll be nearing the Leviathan's lair soon. Tell the men to be ready."

Keenan nodded and turned to leave when the wizard stepped in front of him, a crooked grin playing on his lips as his eyes fell on me. *Where had he come from?* He wore a pair of dark breeches and a forest green tunic that frayed along the seams. Unkempt blonde hair whisked in the breeze, and I had to bite back the desire to squirm under his devious grin.

"A word, Arie—"

Keenan moved so fast I barely saw the dagger that hovered inches from the wizard's throat. "That's Captain to you, *Wizard*."

"Ooo, threatening a wizard, you must have a death wish." The wizard's smile grew as he brought his attention toward me. "*Captain* Arie."

My heart nearly slipped from my chest as the two of them stared each other down. Keenan was no match against the wizard, and he knew it. While I appreciated his valiant effort at demanding respect for his captain, I would much prefer him alive than the alternative. "Keenan, back down."

He lowered his dagger, his hand visibly shaking as he walked away. I wasn't sure if it was from adrenaline or fear.

The king had forced the wizard on me, and his presence had put all of us on edge. The horrible things he'd done were whispered in all the dark places of Khan. *The king's weapon.* Used as a torturer, sometimes as a barrier against his enemies. All of it was speculation, of course. I'd never seen his work up close and personal. I supposed I would so long as he was here. Now he wanted to speak with me when I'd rather he stayed below deck and rot. "What can I do for you, Wizard?"

"I have a name."

It didn't matter what his real name was because once this was all over, he'd be off my ship, and I'd never have to see him again. "I'm sure it's a lovely name. Now if you don't mind—"

The wizard didn't relent. "I just figured that since we got off on the wrong foot, maybe—"

"Got off on the wrong foot? You and King Roland are why we're sailing straight into the hornet's nest. But sure, tell me how you're going to make that all better with your words, W*izard*."

"I have simply come here to offer my help."

"Why did the king *really* send you? If he's worried this is a death sentence, surely he can't spare the great and powerful Wizard of Khan. And I don't believe it's because he thinks I'll try to break my sister out."

"The king has his reasons."

"You have no idea, do you?"

"Do you need help, or not?" he snarled.

With death looming over all our heads, I needed all the help I could get, but I wouldn't give him the satisfaction of admitting that.

I spread my arms out. "Do I *look* like I need help?"

"If we're being forced to work together, the least you can do is be nice to the only one who can keep you and your crew alive."

The idea of needing *anyone* to help keep me alive stung, but he was right; for my sister to live, the wizard had to make it back in one piece. It didn't stop me from thinking about all the ways I wanted to watch him bleed.

Leaving the helm, I slid Slayer from the strap on my hip and twirled it in my hand until I was inches from him. His grin faltered for a brief second as he lowered his gaze to Slayer's blade. I pressed it to his chest and looked into his eyes.

"What is with you and your crew and the need for pointy things. I promise I come in peace." He winked, and I wanted to squirm. He may be scary and full of power, but this was *my* ship, and I wouldn't allow him to think of me as weak. Flecks of gold shimmered in his good eye as something warm wrapped itself around my wrist. I glanced down, but there was nothing there, yet the pulse of heat grew within seconds. Was he doing this?

"What are you doing?"

"Well, it's only fair that I threaten you, too, don't you think?"

I hesitated as the warmth traveled down my arm. What kind of magic was this? I wasn't sure, but I had no intentions of finding out. I lowered the dagger and the heat around my wrists dissipated.

"Let's get one thing straight. If anything, and I mean *anything*, happens to my sister? I am holding you personally responsible." A raging fire plumed inside of me; heat rose in every crevice as I gripped Slayer tighter. "And no, I won't be civil to a pathetic piece of work like you. Kidnapping innocent girls from their beds for a bit of gold? They say sea creatures are monsters. Threaten me all you want, but you will leave my crew alone."

Loud voices from below pulled me from our conversation. I turned around to find Keenan rushing toward whatever was going on. I followed after him; not bothering to give the wizard a second glance until he grabbed my arm.

"It's Pascal, by the way."

"I'm sorry?"

"My name, little dove," he cooed.

I groaned, tugging my arm from his grasp. I needed to get as far from him as I could, or I'd probably regret what I'd do next. The shouting intensified as I slipped past him and spotted several men gathered in a semi-circle around two others. They hollered and shoved one another until I pushed my way to the center.

"What in the name of Atlantis is going on here?"

"Nathaniel seems to think he can just get away with not paying me," grumbled Hector, a smaller man with broad shoulders, a balding head, and beautiful dark skin that I envied. Pale skin and the pirate life weren't always a good mix. He was hustling a kingsman in a card game the first time we met. The pirate nearly lost his head when the kingsman found out. Lucky for him I knew a thing or two about playing cards.

"I won fair and square," hollered Nathaniel. He towered over me like a giant. His long red hair and thick burly beard were braided with jewels at the ends. He wore a dark tunic that clung to every muscle and trousers that showed more than just the strength of his legs.

"You two asshats are complaining about gold when we're about to sail into a storm to kill the Leviathan?" No one dared move as the weight of my words fell. They all knew what our mission was and came willingly. My crew had my back just as much as I did theirs, but that didn't mean squabbles didn't happen.

"Keenan, handle this," I said. "Everyone else back to their stations!"

I waved a hand of dismissal and headed for my quarters. It was where I kept the information that would hopefully keep us all alive.

There wasn't much known about the Leviathan, because only a select few had ever come out of Scarlett's Lagoon mostly unscathed. Those who did either went insane or became hellbent on its death. Then again, I didn't recall Captain Hook being either and he was the only pirate I personally knew who'd gone up against it.

Captain Hook. Just thinking his name felt wrong. We'd been rivals for as long as I'd been a hunter, stealing each other's bounties and treasures along the way. However he managed to escape the beast was information I wished I had.

Leaving the men to guide us to the lagoon, I found my way to the sanctuary that I'd called my home for nearly a decade. The space consisted of everything I owned. A large desk sat at the far end where books and scrolls lay scattered across its surface. Opposite that was my bed, a chest of clothes, and other small trinkets. My cabinet remained closed, but inside was a plethora of fine weaponry from all over the seven seas, things I had collected during bounties or stolen while boarding enemy ships.

But all of that—the furniture and trinkets—were nothing compared to my trophy collection. Heads of various sea creatures hung on every viable space of the walls that surrounded me. All varying in size, from the small water sprites that were as small as my own head, to the large sea serpents that would make a lion cower in fear. I approached my favorite trophy: a sea serpent with long horns protruding from the top that spiraled to the back. Jagged teeth that had left a scar along my thigh. Green ombre scales shimmered along its head, and a pair of onyx eyes bore into me, so clear that I could see my reflection. These same eyes had stared me down as I'd severed the beast's head.

This was never my plan. Becoming a hunter wasn't something I aspired to be. Hells, I didn't even enjoy taking down sea creatures. When this journey began, it led me on a wild chase with little to no leads. Whoever killed my fathers hid themself so well it was as if they were a ghost. The longer I searched the more dead ends I ran into and the more money I lost. Anyone who'd heard rumors spent their time lecturing me about how a young girl wasn't meant to live a life of vengeance rather than what I wanted to know. It's how I met Keenan, the first hunter I'd ever met. It was also how I became a captain. He'd taught me this life, showed me what it could do for me and my cause. Though, so far, even a life at sea produced nothing besides a resentful sister.

This had started as a way to make money, with each bounty I was able to acquire a crew and search the seas for my fathers' killer. These mounts on the walls were reminders of why I kept pushing forward and why I needed to do this. A split second of sadness rushed its way forward and I swallowed it down. These monster's deaths were simply a means to an end.

Slipping my dagger from its sheath, I twirled it in my hand. *The Monster Slayer*. My personal weapon of choice. It was larger than most daggers and its blade was sharper than anything I'd ever held. Its edge curved like the body of the same serpent who hung before me. The ornate hilt had been carved by my hand—a dragon, tail curling down to the butt end and stopping at a hidden compartment. I pressed a finger to the base of the tail, revealing an even smaller blade. I couldn't recall how much blood Slayer had tasted over the years, but none had been sweeter than the beady-eyed serpent before me.

Returning to my desk, I placed Slayer on its surface and flopped in my chair. Every scrap of paper scattered before me contained bits of information about every creature I—or any other hunter—had come across. Each piece was gold to a monster hunter. My fingers scanned through them until stopping on the one I needed.

The Leviathan: a sea dragon like no other, who dwelled in a cave on Scarlett's Lagoon. All the depictions showed a monster of giant proportions with dozens of tentacles protruding from a long winding tail. Some texts said that it had armored skin making it difficult to kill, while others said it was impossible to get near due to its ability to boil the surrounding water. For those who weren't so fortunate to escape, the monster left nothing but battered ships and bones. Out of everything known about the beast, one thing was certain.

It was *deadly*.

I took a deep breath; we were about to either confirm or debunk these texts as we sailed closer to its lair. I just hoped we would come out of it alive.

A knock sounded at my door and I jumped. "It's me," Keenan called. "You'd better get out here."

I groaned at the interruption and left my quarters. On deck, lacerating rain poured from the sky, assaulting both me and the ship. It was nothing compared to the threat of the waves that rose like a tsunami around us. Where had this storm come from? I ran to the helm, noticing Giles furrowed brow as his face strained against the storm. His fiery red hair clung to his face while his black shirt and pants were soaked. He hadn't been with my crew long, but he was a great sailor with a keen sense of direction.

"Go help the others. I'll take over."

Giles's shoulders sagged as he wiped his brow and joined the rest of the crew, leaving me to keep *Black Betty* upright. I settled in for the dance.

The splash of water combined with the haunting thunder and flashes of lightning swirled around me in a perfect symphony. I ran a hand over my dance partner, feeling the weathered wood beneath my palms as we swayed in time with the storm's mighty tempo. While the sea thrashed, we waltzed over its waves in perfect rhythm. Adrenaline pumped through my veins, blood pounded in my ears, and even though fear nipped at the back of my neck, it didn't take away from the rush that surged within me.

This was where I belonged.

As we rocked against the waves, the men on deck hustled to keep us upright. The *Betty* was a fine vessel, a ship that had never failed, and with me as its captain, it would sail the seven seas until my last breath. Because when I died, this ship would go down with me.

With a crack, lightning struck one of the masts, setting it ablaze. I yelled to Hector, who stood closest, to take the wheel and ran for the mast. Red and yellow flames licked at the wood as the fire crawled toward me. I threw my hands upward, forcing the rain to focus on the fire. The assault drenched me from head to toe, but I refused to let up. Power surged through me, coursing through my veins as rain and fire battled one another. The rain was clearly the victor as it overwhelmed the fire, but as one fire ended another started. I pushed more of my gift into the clouds, and the rain intensified. Finally, after what felt like hours rather than minutes, the fire ceased.

For years I'd been practicing my powers—a gift from the gods granted to those who were worthy of wielding such a power. Or that's what I'd read. When I first started learning about my gift, I came across a book that gave me a little insight into what was going on. I was a sea witch. The second I'd touched the water, the same water my fathers never wanted me to go near, I'd felt it. Raw and potent. It was then that I began teaching myself to wield the magic inside. After much practice, I found I could use the sea and storms to my advantage, and so I did.

"We're the luckiest ship on the seven seas to have you as our captain, Arie." Keenan slapped my back as he passed. I shook my head, a smile tugging on my lips.

"Captain, look!" Sanders stood over the rail and pointed toward what my gift told me should have been the eye of the storm. Instead, the sea had an eerie calmness save for the clouds that continued to flash and boom with fury above us. Somehow, the storm couldn't reach the island.

Scarlett's Lagoon. We'd reached the beast's dwelling.

But that wasn't the worst of it.

"Is that what I think it is?" Keenan asked, head tilted toward the water.

I rushed to the ship's rail. A river of crimson trailed to hundreds of lifeless bodies as far as the eye could see—not just bodies, but luminescent skeletons. Victims of the Leviathan; all of them glowed yellow like thousands of fluttering fireflies. I'd never seen such a thing and it had my heart hammering in my chest as we sailed on. I knew the beast was fearsome and it left destruction in its wake, but it was something else entirely to gaze upon it.

"It's what happens when souls are taken from their body. When a soul doesn't pass on." Pascal appeared next to me and I jumped. For sea's sake, did he just appear out of thin air? His eyes scanned the sea. "Their bones will float along the surface of the water until their souls cross over. It's part of the magic that binds a soul and its body together."

Those poor men, to not be able to pass on to the afterlife. It left a sour taste in my mouth and an ache in my chest. Not only was there death, but the wreckage of ships made any naval war look like child's play. Where there wasn't a skeleton, there floated pieces of other ships, wooden barrels, or torn fabric. We were sailing right into a graveyard for the Leviathan's victims. If a monster could do all of this? I shuddered. Could a sea witch take on such a fearsome beast?

"All right, Pascal, let's see what you can do about getting us safely to the island."

It was time to see if the wizard could be useful. It would also help to know the extent of his power as we neared the Leviathan's island. I wondered then whether it was the wizard or the Leviathan that had me so on edge. As I stared at the death and destruction, I listened to the whispers of the crew. They must have felt it too.

We were sailing straight into the monster's den, and not a soul would survive.

III. DEVIL'S DEN

AS THE STORM CLEARED, WE SEARCHED THE WATER FOR signs of the Leviathan. Scarlett's shoreline wasn't far now and thanks to Pascal's magic, *Black Betty* had disappeared from sight. He'd assured me that no one, not even the beast, would see the ship. As much as it pained me to say so, I was grateful to have a wizard on board.

For now.

Restless waves stroked the rocky sand as we approached. The air was pungent with the taste of salt. At the edge of the beach, a line of trees stretched for miles and beyond that the Leviathan's cave. My heart thudded in my chest as the men dropped anchor and prepared the rowboats.

I'd done my best to prepare us for anything. I'd use my gift to the best of my ability, but it was hard to know what weaknesses the Leviathan had. Slayer would only get me so far. I swapped my sword for a pistol and had Hector make everyone a round of hunter bullets. I never asked what he used to make them, but they packed one hell of a punch and had gotten me out of a few sticky situations. I just hoped it would be enough.

Having Pascal gave us a bigger advantage. While my magic pulled on the sea and storm, his appeared to come from something deeper than that. Wherever it came from didn't matter, what did was how effective it would be. From the small displays of it, and personal experience, I knew he'd be an asset.

And, if we fell, those who stayed on the ship were to use whatever means necessary to finish the job. One way or another we were going to end this or die trying.

When we made it to shore, I turned to those who'd be risking their lives for me, for my sister. Twenty of the finest fighters of the seven seas awaited my command. A bunch of burley misfits that had been with me for so long they'd become my family. My eyes scanned over the crowd and my stomach fluttered as my nerves worsened. They were all counting on me to lead them as they always did, but this time there was a threat unlike anything we've faced before. I sighed, pulling on my strength before clearing my throat.

"Before we go any further, I want to thank you all for coming. For stepping up and risking your lives for this mission. I know we've been there before, but this time is different. This time we are up against a beast like no other, a fight that we may not come back from. However, with my magic and the wizard's help, I'm confident we can come out victorious." I paused and looked at the group of misfits who stood before me. *My* misfits. Even though the odds were stacked against us, I'd gladly run into the fire with these men. The same group of bloodthirsty pirates I'd spent countless nights swapping stories with and schooling in poker. Our bodies bore the same scars from our travels, all of us having put our lives on the line for one another. We knew how to work as one unit, but this wasn't just any hunt for a sea serpent or a hydra.

Not everyone would walk away from this mission.

"Just know that I won't judge anyone who wishes to stay on this beach."

Hector stepped forward. "You've sacrificed more for us than anyone else. You saved each and every one of us from a fate worse than death. If you choose to walk into the den of a fearless monster, I *will* walk beside you."

A murmur of agreement cut across the group as they all took a step closer. I nodded in thanks, knowing that if I spoke the tears I held back would tumble in waves.

Each of them raised their swords. "For the sea, for the captain!"

They erupted in cheer, continuing to chant as they walked into the unknown. I shook my head, a smile tugging at my lips. They were all crazy, and yet they were mine.

"Remember, we don't know what's in store for us here. This is new territory on all fronts so keep your wits, and blades, close. Any sign of movement or the beast, just give a whistle."

"I hope you know what you're doing." Pascal's voice was a whisper in my ear, and I jumped, whirling around to find him gazing at the trees behind us. He grabbed my arm and pulled me until my face was inches from his. Gooseflesh trailed down my arms as mint and something sweet wafted through my nostrils. "We may have made it this far, but I feel something wrong with this place. Something… wrong. Something wrong."

He kept repeating himself as if he were broken, wide-eyed as he scanned the forest. I tried not to notice the crazed man lurking behind his dark eyes and yanked from his grasp.

"If you grab me one more time, I will shove—"

"Yes, yes, you will go stabby-stab. I get it." He rolled his eyes before trotting off toward the trees.

"Let's move." I hung back as the rest of the crew followed Keenan. He was a great navigator when it came to unfamiliar terrain. Hells, if it weren't for him, I'd still be roaming through the forest back in Khan trying to find my way back to the city. He'd found me, only a few months after my fathers' death, alone and hungry as I followed what would be another dead end. I'd failed to find the killer and was ready to give up when he'd offered to help. We'd spent the next few hours trudging through the dense trees talking about whatever sprang to mind.

I didn't realize until later that he hadn't even asked me about why I was out there to begin with.

I waited until the last man walked past before taking up the rear. Unease washed over me, sending gooseflesh down my arms. Being here had me on edge, yes, but the faint prick at the back of my neck and the hair that stood on end had me on high alert. The Leviathan, while able to travel on land and sea, could be out here waiting for the right moment to strike.

I knew from the text that it was large. How large, I wasn't sure. We were already working with little knowledge, and the further we moved inland the worse my nerves got. I opened my mouth to speak but closed it for fear that a quake in my voice would expose my trepidation.

Shoving my shaking hands into my pockets, I tried to ignore the ache that crawled its way through my body and wondered if Pascal sensed the same impending doom that I did. His continued skipping made me think otherwise. Either that or he was better at hiding it.

Those in front of me scanned the surrounding trees for anything out of the ordinary, some of them murmuring their worries to one another. I didn't like eavesdropping, but there was so much silence in the air it was impossible to not hear their concerns.

The wind wailed between distorted trunks, carrying the sickly stink of wood rot. Around us, the canopy of spruce trees grew sparser and before long we stood beneath ragged, bare branches, leaves littering the ground and crunching under our boots. The island was otherwise quiet. There were no birds circling above, or signs of antler marks on trees, or bear tracks in the dirt. Not even the trees held any sign that animals lived in them. It was as if all life had ceased to exist. Had the beast scared them all away… or eaten them?

Deeper unease crept along my skin, and I knew at that moment Pascal was right, something was very wrong here.

An involuntary shiver escaped, and I pulled Slayer from my hip. The pistol on my other hip would have been more sufficient, but my dagger was my lifeline. When I held her, the sense of safety covered me like a warm blanket.

"Captain!" Keenan yelled from the front of our group who'd stopped in their tracks and craned their necks to see what was going on. I rushed past them and stilled.

More death. More destruction.

Fallen trees littered the ground, flattened like flowers pressed inside the pages of a book. In the center stood a large hill, and not just any hill, but one made of hundreds of bones, all of them glowing yellow like the ones at sea. Pascal had said these were the bones of those whose souls were taken, those who couldn't pass on.

Magic pulsed through the air akin to my beating heart. As though the island itself was eating up the magic the soulless bones left behind. I looked at the men who stood at its base, some of them had gone ghostly pale while others crossed their arms over their chest with pursed lips. What was going through their heads? Were they worried they'd end up with the same fate?

Bringing my focus back to the pile, I wondered how many of my fellow hunters had died here? Were they all human? I wasn't sure how to tell but one thing became clear, these poor souls would roam the world, never able to rest until someone did something. Until *I* did something.

Hector strolled forward and bent down to get a closer look. He kept his hands and feet away from the bones, but I could see the way the wheels turned in his mind as he mulled over what he was seeing.

His gaze rose to meet mine. "No skulls."

I joined him, getting a better view of the pile. Femurs and various arm bones were sprinkled amongst rib cages and pelvic bones. Some were whole, while others remained broken beyond identification. Dozens of other tiny bones I assumed had once been fingers and toes littered the ground nearest me. Were those teeth marks? I refused to pick one up to be certain, but the odd scraping marks seemed to be done by something sharp. Unless the skulls were hidden on the bottom, Hector was right, all the skulls were missing.

I couldn't let this stand. The amount of energy that coursed through these bones rumbled in my own. It was as if their pain and suffering surrounded me in a rush of emotion. My knees threatened to buckle as I sucked in a deep breath. The men around me kneeled around the pile, all of us bowing our heads to honor the sacrifices of the lives lost.

We all felt it, but it was so much more than the pain and suffering. If anyone with the smallest hint of magic came across these bones they'd be able to harness its power and I refused to let that stand. No one would gain from these deaths.

"Stand back." I called out, waiting as the men backed away from the pile, all their eyes pinned on me as I opened my awareness. My magic's unrelenting force built and built until a jolt of lightning split the sky.

Above, darkened clouds formed, rolling in like the tide.

I threw my hands up and called to the clouds. I'd learned long ago that a sea witch's power was built much like a storm. As though my powers and the strength of the weather were one in the same. From each explosion to every flash of light, I wielded it like it belonged to me. The clouds answered with a crack of thunder as lightning ignited the pile of bone. It wouldn't help the poor souls cross over, but at least this way no one else would gain from their deaths. I wanted to fall to my knees and weep for them, instead I settled on killing the bastard that did this.

I turned to my men. "Let's end this."

"To the Devil's den!" yelled Keenan.

The beast's den was carved out of a large mountainside that stretched hundreds of feet into the sky. Several of the surrounding trees lay smashed and broken as though the beast had knocked them over. Drops of water slid down the rocky walls and a cool breeze wrapped itself around me. We stood outside the massive cave, hidden by the remaining trees while we waited for signs of the beast's presence.

"It appears you will need to go inside to meet the Leviathan." Pascal stepped through the crowd to stand next to me. "Standing out here is only prolonging the inevitable."

I scowled. "Would *you* like to take the first step toward death?"

"Death *is* inevitable." He raised a brow before leaving the group and heading into the cave. I let him go. If the beast was right inside, he would be its first victim. At least then I wouldn't have to worry about killing the wizard myself. It wouldn't be my fault if he was eaten. Surely the king wouldn't punish Frankie for a freak accident... or so I hoped.

Then again, where *was* the Leviathan? If not at sea and not roaming its island, it had to be inside, but shouldn't it have heard us by now? I had imagined fighting the beast with the trees for cover. Now we were heading into its den, and I had no exact plan of attack.

"I swear there's something not right with that guy." Keenan shook his head as he came to stand beside me.

"Are we going to follow him?" asked Nathaniel.

"Of course," I tilted my head in his direction. "We didn't come all this way to sit around with our thumbs up our asses. I'd just rather Pascal be the one to die first."

I looked away and pleaded once again to the celestial beings that I didn't believe in. *Almighty gods, have mercy on my men.*

Whatever awaited us inside, I just hoped they would survive. The air around me was thick with their tension. Some fidgeted with their coats while others paced along the open space. Some spoke in hushed tones and yet all I could do was stare at the cave's opening. At any moment Pascal, or the Leviathan, could come billowing out the hole like a bull seeing red. A few minutes passed before Pascal emerged from the cave, waving for us to follow.

The beast's den had just enough light to see dim outlines, but not enough to reveal all its secrets. A cold draft swept through the cave as we traveled inward, and my heart picked up its pace.

"You think the beast is even in here?" Keenan's gaze traveled over the cave before settling on me.

I shrugged. "I don't know, but something doesn't feel right."

Turning to the rest of the men I said, "Watch your step and stick close. No one goes anywhere alone."

"Wouldn't the beast have made itself known by now?" asked Nathaniel.

"Unless it's hiding," answered Sanders, the crew's medic.

While the men speculated, I gripped Slayer tighter in hopes of keeping my hands from trembling.

The massive cave was covered in glowing worms, blue and green colors scattered across the rock. Their light granted the cave enough illumination to see our surroundings. It was better than having to carry torches. I didn't want to be caught unguarded here and the light would only attract unwanted attention.

Stalactites hung from the ceiling like icicles waiting to strike at any given notice, but it was the stalagmites that had me checking my footing. Where Pascal stood, two boulders hid the entrance to a side passage. His hands spread out at his sides as he bent down to press one of them to the ground. A zap of static rolled over my skin like gooseflesh.

"I believe the beast's nest is just beyond this formation." He gestured for us to move forward. "I'm not sensing any presence inside, but with little knowledge of what the beast can do, let's be sure to stay on our toes."

Stepping around Pascal, I led the way through the passage, all the while wondering how a massive dragon could fit through such a tiny space. Magic? Was there a backdoor to this place? All questions were answered the second I entered the den.

Blinding light beamed down from above, the storm nowhere to be seen as the cave's ceiling opened to reveal a cloudless sky. There was magic here; I could sense it with every step, feel it as it cascaded down my arms and torso to meet at my toes. Every fiber of my being ignited with urgency and need—the magic calling me home. Maybe the Leviathan could wield magic. It would explain a few things. Ignoring the desire to let my own powers unleash, I readied myself for an attack that never came.

The cave was empty.

"Is it hunting?" Keenan asked.

"If it were, we'd already be its dinner," murmured one of the others. My men were scattered around the cave, scouring for whatever we could find. If the Leviathan wasn't here maybe the cargo would be. Leaving them to it, I took to exploring.

This part of the cave was much like the entrance. The same rocky icicles and luminescent worms, though that wasn't what held my attention. Along the wall, thousands of skulls sat on what appeared to be a shelf carved into the cave. The shelf circled the entire room and spiraled upward until it reached the top.

Why would such a beast do something like this? Most of the monsters I've killed were simple-minded, yet something told me the Leviathan was much more than that. There were cultures that sacrificed some of their horde to appease gods, but this didn't quite feel that way. Thousands of bones had been discarded like trash, if someone were to sacrifice people, surely, they would sacrifice the entire body. What would someone gain from keeping the skulls? I walked over to one of the shelves, their hollowed eyes peering at me as though they pleaded for my help. All these poor souls that had died for what?

There was more to this beast than I realized. To not only create a sort of shrine made of skulls, but to have the ability to display them like…

Trophies.

I swallowed, taking slow, methodical steps backward. Isn't that what I did? Did I not collect the skulls of my kills and display them in my quarters? This was different, monsters kill the innocent. I had to tell myself that, had to believe it or what would this make me? Was I a monster, too?

When I hung a monster's head on my wall, I did it as a reminder. A way for me to look back at why I did what I did. The mounts on my walls were simply a memento to remind me of my mission—to find the murderous son of a bitch who killed the fathers who'd given me everything.

I rubbed a shaky hand over my face and inhaled. A wave of acid welled up in my stomach and I fought the urge to turn and bolt. My men were counting on me to stay strong, to be their leader. I took in a few more laggard breaths before pushing on. On the far side of the cave, a giant nest made of twigs and leaves had been tucked into a small alcove. I searched for the king's stolen cargo, but there was nothing here besides death and sand and rock.

"The beast isn't here, and it doesn't look like there are any signs of where it went." I ran a hand through my hair. "Let's head back to the ship and maybe we can wait for it to return. There's no sense in being here when it returns." I waited as my men piled out of the room and back toward the entrance. As I turned to search for Pascal, something that sounded like cannon fire boomed in the distance. I braced myself against one of the walls as the floor vibrated. Pascal surged from where he was kneeling, whirling around until his eyes locked on mine.

"What—?"

Another blast sounded, only much louder this time. Chunks of rock fell from the walls. I dodged what I could, but debris still sprayed me. Stalactites broke from the ceiling, crashing to the ground. I ran toward the middle of the room; the opening above would keep me from getting pierced by one.

I'd nearly made it to the center when another crash had me dropping to the floor, unable to dodge the shrapnel. Before I could get up, Pascal shoved me, sending me rolling toward the Leviathan's nest. My arm cracked as I hit something hard, and I cried out. Pain radiated through my arm and over my shoulder as I turned to find Pascal laying where I had just been, pinned under a stalactite. I surged to my feet, ignoring the pain in my arm, and ran to him. He was still breathing, but a deep gash oozed crimson.

Taking a deep breath, I pushed the stalactite off him to find no other wounds. I grabbed him and pulled toward the nest, hoping that the small cove would keep him safe. Not that I really cared if he wasn't hurt. He only had to make it back alive, not uninjured. I reached for Slayer, but it was no longer at my hip. I drew my pistol instead and walked toward the pathway we'd entered through, but there was no way out. Fallen rock blocked the entrance and we were pinned down.

"Keenan?" I cried out.

"Cap, are you okay?"

"I'm fine, but it looks like we're trapped in here. Can you guys get out?"

"Yeah, but I'm not—"

"Yes, you will." Keenan wouldn't leave me. Not unless I forced him to, and I wasn't about to allow any of my men to die trying to get me out of here. "I'm a sea witch, remember, I will find a way out. Make sure the *Betty* and the rest of our men are okay."

I didn't give him a chance to respond before I was making my way back to Pascal who'd begun to stir.

He *saved* me, and had risked his own life for mine.

"Why did you push me out of the way?" I crossed my arms. "Aren't you the one who said death is inevitable?"

Blood and dirt and sweat covered his face, yet he still smiled. I narrowed my eyes on the wound that was healed and no longer oozed.

"Your death would simply mean the king would send someone else to fetch his precious cargo. I, for one, would like to make this the last and final trip. So I need you alive."

I narrowed my eyes. "Did you heal yourself?"

Pascal dusted himself off and stood. "Magic is mysterious, isn't it?"

There wasn't time to question him further, so I kept to what was necessary. "Right, well we're trapped here and by the sounds of it my ship is attacking. Which either means the Leviathan is out there, or an enemy ship. We need to find a way out. Now."

"The only way is up, little dove."

Up meant having to climb. The rows of shelves along the wall would provide us with an escape, but it also meant having to stare into the faces of the Leviathan's victims. There wasn't another option, not if I wanted to get to my ship and my men.

I found Slayer underneath a pile of rock and stuck it back in its home before moving toward the shelves.

"Is your arm all right?" Pascal asked.

In the chaos, I'd nearly forgotten about my arm. I lifted it and instantly regretted it. Hissing, I bite my tongue. "I think it's broken." How in the *hells* was I going to climb with one arm?

Pascal walked over to me, and I stepped away, not wanting him anywhere near me.

"Do you want me to heal you, or not?" he snapped.

I opened my mouth when another bang had the walls shaking once more. Stifling my pride, I held out my broken arm, a whimper escaping my lips. I didn't have time to let my damned pride get in the way. My men were in trouble.

"This is going to sting." Pascal grabbed my arm in his, his hands soft and warm as heat wrapped around the wound. "Not broken, but I imagine you'd still have a hard time climbing." He pressed harder against my skin and my arm numbed, as if it had never been hurt in the first place. Gooseflesh flowed down my arms and legs. The warmth washed over me and then quickly dissipated leaving me crying out in pain. My breath caught in my throat, and I lurched away from him. He let go, and the pain subsided. My eyes traveled to his. He stared at me, his face flush and hands trembling. Was he okay?

Why the hells did I care if he was okay?

"How did you do that?"

"You of all people should know." Pascal backed away from me and shifted to look at the hole in the ceiling. "Now, shall we ascend the great wall of death?"

We moved together, one hand and foot at a time as we shimmied our way up. He moved ahead leaving me to watch as he climbed. Small bits of rock broke off, and I swallowed hard, climbing freely without a rope had my heart racing. Yet Pascal didn't seem to mind. I found myself in awe of how easily he shifted from one rock to another. He was a natural, moving with such grace and precision it seemed as if he climbed every day of his life.

We emerged from the hole a few minutes later and I sucked in every bit of fresh air that I could and laughed. I may not have killed the Leviathan, but I made it out of its den alive. "Thank the gods for small favors," I muttered.

"Are you good?" Pascal asked, his hand outstretched. I took it and hoisted myself up and out of the cave.

"Yeah, I think so." I looked at Pascal and opened my mouth to thank him when his eyes widened as they wandered somewhere behind me.

I slowly turned to see a ship, not *Black Betty*, just off the coast of the island. All three of its masts were on fire and I could only make out a small part of the flag, but I knew whose ship that was.

"*The Marauder.*"

Captain Hook's ship sat out in the middle of the sea with its masts ablaze. I sighed in relief. It wasn't my ship, but why the *hells* was he out there to begin with? What had he been firing at? Part of me wanted nothing more than to sit here and watch it burn. If he burned up at sea, who else would I steal from? No one else played our game the way he did.

"*Shit*," I groaned, "we have to help them."

"Arie, we don't have time—"

"For all we know, the Leviathan could be attacking him. Plus, I won't let a ship go down when I could have saved it. No matter who's her captain."

IV. SIREN'S SONG

"REMIND ME AGAIN WHY WE'RE SAILING TO SAVE THIS man and his ship?" Keenan grumbled, sweat dripping down his brow as we ran back to *Black Betty*.

They'd been trying to dig through the rubble when Pascal and I emerged from behind them. The cause of the cave-in had been Captain Hook's cannons. I shook my head, something seemed off. Hook had once sailed through these parts and came out unscathed. So why in all the seven seas was he trying to do it again?

Everyone piled into the boats and rowed toward our ship. Getting to Hook was the priority right now and with luck, we would reach him before his ship sank. Climbing aboard the *Betty*, I gave the orders needed and made my way up the mainmast, my arms clinging to the ropes as I shimmied my way up until I reached the top.

From clear skies, I called the storm. I didn't usually have to stand in any particular spot, but from up here at least I could get a better view. A spark ignited at the ends of my fingertips as I pushed my magic front and center. Darkened clouds gathered in a swirl as light streaked the sky. As my magic built, the storm intensified and answered with a deafening roar. Rain pattered from the sky as the fire on Hook's ship rose to meet it. They clashed against one another; a fight easily won by the rain—proving to be a stronger foe.

We made our way around the bay and found the rest of *The Marauder*. Screams carried over the waves and nearly brought me to my knees. Pain and anguish filled those voices and with every bit of energy I had, I called to the sea below and asked for its aid.

A swell built and built until it rose above the *Betty*. The giant wave picked up the ship like a broom picking up dirt, sweeping us closer to Hook and his men. It brought us down with a force that, if not for my own magic, would have smashed *Black Betty* into little bits.

Now that we were close, the screams grew louder and more coherent. But the Leviathan was nowhere in sight. From the top of the mast, I looked into the sea's depths and found nothing but rocky waves and…

Something moved beneath the surface; perhaps it was as simple as a shark, yet the shape seemed more human than that. A soft hum drowned out the cries of Hook's men—the voice was so sweet and inviting that I wanted nothing more than to get lost in the melody. I closed my eyes, letting the song build inside of me.

Memories of a home once lost flooded my vision. My fathers, both of them together again as they sat in their favorite chairs beside a lit fireplace. Frankie lay next to them, a book in her hand as she lost herself in a new world.

My heart warmed and the euphoria of seeing this life filled me with joy. I opened my arms to welcome them back when a *boom* shattered my memory.

Back to reality, and with an aching heart. My fathers were dead, and my sister was locked away. Those memories were just that, and I promised to never forget it.

I looked down to call Keenan in warning, but all my men had stopped working. Instead, they piled as close to the edge of the ship as they could, their eyes closed as they swayed with the voice that had taken me. A voice I'd heard only once before during a hunt. This wasn't the sea that called, nor was it the Leviathan that had them enthralled.

"*Fucking* sirens!"

I scurried down the mast as fast as my limbs allowed and grabbed ahold of the man closest to me. Weston, the ship's chef, and a good man with a heart of gold. His eyes were glossed over like the fog of the storm and no matter how hard I shook him, he remained enthralled.

If I didn't fix this soon, all my men would tumble to the sea and be swept away by sirens.

"Not today, you murderous wenches!"

I threw my hands up to the clouds above and sent a strike of lightning into the water. It gave just enough of a jolt to stop the music and allow my men to gain back their consciousness.

"Find something to plug your ears. There are sirens in the water."

Men scrambled around me, searching for whatever they could jam into their ears. As long as it drowned out the siren's song, they'd be safe. I'd read that sirens catered more toward men, yet, I still refused to take that chance. I tore a piece of fabric from my shirt, then into two, and I shoved each one into my ears just as the sirens started their song once more.

"Keenan, spyglass!" I nudged him, holding up my hand to curl around my eye in hopes he could decipher what I meant.

Seconds later it landed in my hand, and I pulled it up to see nothing but chaos. The masts were smoldering and ashes rained down.

"You don't suppose they torched their own masts to keep the sirens back, do you? Or maybe it was something else," I said, only to realize no one could hear me.

Returning my attention to the fight, dozens of sirens raided the ship, throwing and tossing men overboard. From this distance, some of his men had managed to cover their ears and I sighed in relief. No one deserved a siren's death. Not even my enemy.

I motioned toward Hector and Nathaniel and tapped my back. Both nodded and I was grateful we had all spent so much time together. There were never questions, only loyalty, only trust. We'd hunted monsters and rival pirates alike and through all of that, we'd learned how each other moved. We were family.

Both men tapped their backs in return, signaling that we would look out for one another.

Keenan had managed to bring the *Betty* so close that it nearly touched *The Marauder*. While a few others worked on securing the ropes, Hector, Nathaniel, and I loaded up on weaponry. I adjusted my hat and grabbed a rope.

I sought out Hook and swore when I spotted him, surrounded by sirens. His raven black hair tousled and wet against his face—a pistol at his feet. The tip of his sword pointed to the oncoming threat while his other hand—well, hook—fended off a siren to his left. His brows furrowed, nearly fusing together. Part of his shirt lay open and ripped, revealing a chiseled chest. I cleared my throat and returned the spyglass to Keenan.

The number of remaining men dwindled by the minute.

I nodded once more to Hector and Nathaniel, who held their own ropes, before jumping. In one giant leap, the three of us swung across. Air *whooshed* past me, catching my hair in its grasp. As I landed on the deck, it all came crashing forward in a sea of red.

Around us, the sirens froze, almost as if they'd looked into the eyes of Medusa and been turned to stone. A chill ran down my back as, in unison, heads turned stiffly toward me. Their faces were sunken and hollow. Grotesque mandibles opened to reveal rows of jagged teeth. My books had described sirens as beautiful beings, much like their mermaid counterparts, but these were far from it. I bit back a scream and unleashed Slayer.

Nathaniel fell to all fours, his lips moving but I couldn't make out what he said. He swayed again. One of his ear protections must have fallen out on the way over.

"Hec—"

Hector was already there, throwing his hands over Nathaniel's ears.

"We've been expecting you, Arie the Hunter."

Terror sealed my throat. I couldn't scream. The sirens spoken in the same monotone voice, at the same time. How in the seven seas could I hear them through my ear defenders?

"Wh-what do you want?" I swallowed down the fear bubbling in my stomach.

"We want nothing you can give, only She Who Watches can."

The words were solid in my head, like a whisper that only I could hear. I looked at Hector and Nathaniel, but they simply stared at me with furrowed brows.

"She Who Watches?"

"Yes, yes that's what we said. Are all humans this dumb?" One of the sirens cocked her head at me. She was missing both her eyes and had her hand on the siren next to her.

"Why are you attacking these men if you're here for me?" I asked.

"Delicious snack," said a siren to my left.

"Too good to pass up," said another.

They were slowly losing sync with each other, and I wasn't sure that was any better than them speaking as one. My eyes darted to Hook who was reaching for his pistol like an idiot. I shot him a glare, shaking my head as subtle as possible.

"What," he mouthed, and when I didn't lower my gaze, dropped his arms to his sides. If he wanted to live, he'd be better off backing away and letting me handle this. "Why are you here?"

"You ask many questions. Yet not ones that matter most," cackled another siren to my right.

"Do you always speak in riddles?" Hector mumbled from behind me, his hand pressed firmly to Nathaniel's exposed ear.

All the sirens turned to Hector and hissed like feral cats.

"You can hear them?" I asked.

"What? I can't hear you." Hector pointed to his stuffed ears.

"He hears what we want him to hear," said the blind one.

"She is looking for you." One of them crawled on all fours until she kneeled a couple of feet in front of me.

"Who?"

Before I could get an answer, a gunshot rang out. Black slime spattered my face, the smell of rotten seaweed caught in my nostrils, and I gagged. On the floor nearest me, a siren fell, a hole in the side of her head. The entire ship burst into action. Sirens leaped from all directions as swords were drawn. The rest of my crew landed one after another and in seconds the entire main deck of *The Marauder* was a deadly warzone.

I clutched Slayer, slashing and stabbing my way toward Hook. A siren jumped on his back, its arms around his neck while another pulled on his leg. They were going to try and get him overboard. Get the captain and the rest will fall.

Not on my watch.

I lunged forward and thrust my blade into the siren on Hook's back. It let out a screech, piercing my still-stuffed ears, and I stumbled back. It writhed like a bucking horse as it tried to grab the blade. Thick, black liquid slid down her pale skin. Her hand finally met Slayer's hilt—a finger pressing down on the hidden trigger—and the small blade shot out, piercing her hand. The new wound brought the siren to her knees giving me time to grab Slayer before she fell to the deep below.

Hook was already throwing the siren at his feet overboard when I approached. His ears weren't plugged anymore. Dangerous for him to do such a thing, but I didn't question it.

"Smelling good there, Lockwood." Hook wrinkled his nose. I followed his gaze to my shirt that was covered in black ooze.

"I'm sure I smell better than you look." I scooped his pistol from the ground and handed it to him. Our gazes locked on one another, his eyes trailing down my frame before he snatched his weapon from me. "You good?"

"I don't need your help, so get the *fuck* off my ship." Hook exchanged one weapon for another and threw something behind me. I jumped and twirled to find a small knife jammed in the eye of a siren who stood inches from me. I wanted to squirm. First Pascal saved me, and now Hook. What the *hells* was going on?

Turning back, I scowled and held up my hands. "You almost got me!"

Hook groaned. "Get out of my way."

"You know, if it weren't for me, you'd be in the water with the others."

"If it weren't for *you*"—he stalked over, blue eyes like icy daggers as he pointed his hook at me, —"they wouldn't have been on my ship in the first place."

"Me?" I laughed. "You're the one who sailed to Scarlett's Lagoon."

"Yeah, to kill the Leviathan, not to be attacked by sirens."

I frowned and opened my mouth when a siren jumped toward us from behind a barrel. I threw my arms up to shield myself, but no blow came. Lowering my hands, my gaze drifted toward the *Betty* where Pascal stood, hands outstretched as they glowed a ghostly white. Within seconds, dozens of sirens floated from their hiding places, screeching, and thrashing as Pascal gripped the air around him and pushed his arms apart. The sirens that he'd caught in his trap quit screaming as they were torn in two. More black liquid doused me, this time it covered every inch of me and the air grew putrid. Bile crept its way up my throat and I clamped my mouth shut, not wanting to taste what I was smelling. Pascal moved his hands once more, tossing pieces of siren from *The Marauder*.

Everyone stopped, even the remaining sirens, and we all looked to Pascal whose eyes blazed a bright yellow. I'd never seen such a thing, and to have such power… I knew it was stupid to get on the wizard's bad side, but this, this was madness. It lurked in the crooked smile that played on his lips and the fire that danced in his eyes as he wiped blood from his face. Blood that appeared to be his own.

Was that the price for using his magic? He'd been displaying more of his power since reaching the island.

While Pascal was scarier than any monster I'd come across so far, one thing was certain: he saved me… again. I could have done without being drenched, but I wondered why he was going to such lengths to keep me alive. I knew what he said, that he needed me alive to get this done, but this felt like more than that. Maybe I was looking too much into it, but before I could decide, another shot rang out from somewhere above, pulling my gaze to a man in the crow's nest. A pistol in each hand, he fired at the remaining sirens.

"Atta boy, Smith!" Hook bellowed. His smile widened, displaying a small dimple I hadn't noticed. Then again, I don't think I'd ever seen him smile before.

One siren remind, her eyes wide and terror filled. Instead of turning toward me, she turned to the sea. My chance at finding out who this She Who Watches was dwindled as she ran for the rail.

"Grab her!" I pointed toward the siren in hopes that one of my men could read my lips.

To my delight, Hector released Nathaniel, who found his bearings, and grabbed her. She thrashed against him, her hands and legs flailing, while he wrapped his hand around her mouth. Smart man.

"What do you want me to do with her?" he yelled.

I motioned him over and took the siren's head in my hands, forcing her to look at me. I pulled all of my focus on the eyes that looked back at me, dark as night. Hector released his hold over her mouth.

"Who is She Who Watches?" I pulled on the magic that tied me to the sea and all that dwelled there. Compulsion was finicky and it didn't always work for me. I'd tried it on a nymph years ago and had nearly been crushed by branches from a tree. Who knew nymphs could be so powerful? The magic inside had limits. With luck, the siren wouldn't know what I was doing and it would give me the upper hand.

"She tells us only to find you." The words struggled to come out as she fought against my hold. "We disobeyed."

"What do you mean?"

The siren twisted hard in Hector's grip as she tried to fight the compulsion, my magic straining as he held her tighter. "Only observe, not to approach."

"So why did you?"

A maniacal grin crept on the siren's face as it stopped thrashing. She licked her lips and peered over to Hook, who stood a few feet from us. His arms were crossed and his face still. I had no idea what he was thinking, but when the siren met his eyes, he flinched.

"Ah, right, delicious snack and all." I yanked the siren's head back toward me. "What does she want?"

"To meet her daughter, of course."

Of all the things the siren could have said, that was not one I had been expecting. Her *daughter*, but that would mean… I shook my head. No. My fathers were very clear that my mother died during childbirth. She hadn't survived the trauma. Surely they wouldn't lie to me, not about that. These sirens had the wrong girl.

Before I could ask any more questions, Hook was there with his sword. In one rapid swipe, his blade cut through the siren's neck, severing it before throwing it into the sea.

"What the *fuck*, Hook? I needed her."

"What you need, Lockwood, is to tell me why you're here."

I dropped the headless siren and shoved him back. "Saving your ass."

He took a step forward, but both Hector and Nathaniel flanked me. "No, I meant *here*." Hook gestured around, indicating Scarlett's Lagoon rather than on his ship.

"It's really none of your business."

"It is if you're after the Leviathan."

Why would that matter? I didn't answer him. He could think whatever he wanted, but the Leviathan was mine to kill.

Hook narrowed his eyes and huffed. "You think you stand a chance against it? Stealing treasure and taking on enemy ships is one thing; going up against the Leviathan is like going up against death itself."

"If that were true, you wouldn't be here either," I snarled.

I wanted to tell him that I did more than just those things, that I was capable of more. The Leviathan may be a beast beyond any I've dealt with before, but backing down wasn't an option when it came to saving those I love. I'd face it head on and not give one second thought otherwise. He had no right to tell me I couldn't handle this mission. Ten of him wouldn't stand a chance against the gift that ran through my veins.

Taking a step closer, he pointed his hook at me. The tip hovered inches from me as light reflected off the silvery metal. I glanced up at his eyes and my heart thumped in my chest as heat rose to my cheeks. Without thinking, I leaned into the curve of the hook. I wouldn't allow him to intimidate me.

Hook's brows knitted together. "I've lived to tell my tale. I believe that proves I can best even death. If I were you, I wouldn't get in my way."

Above us the clouds darkened and the hairs on my arms stood on end as static filled the air.

I scoffed. "Get in *your* way. Please, if anyone's getting in anyone's way, it's you. I could be out there searching for the damn thing and instead I decided to save you, and what good did it do me?"

His eyes trailed down to the hook at my chest and he cleared his throat. As he lowered it, his hand balled into a fist. "No one asked you to, and I sure as hell didn't need it."

I turned in a circle, my arms spread outward. "It appears you did." The bickering intensified as did the looming storm, fueled by my anger. I should have let him and his crew die and saved myself all this trouble.

"You're nothing but an ungrateful, narcissist, crocodile—"

"Yeah, well at least—"

"Enough," Keenan bellowed. "This is getting us nowhere." Hook and I stared at each other for a few seconds more before I turned to my first mate. I inhaled, filling my lungs as I centered myself. The clouds dissipated along with my rage.

When no one spoke, he continued. "We need to get out of here, regroup and figure out where to start looking for the Leviathan. Every minute we wait is another minute the Leviathan could be out there wreaking havoc."

This was why Keenan was my right-hand-man. Always the logical one when my temper overshadowed all other thoughts. It hadn't crossed my mind that the Leviathan could be terrorizing the waters. It also had me questioning something else entirely. I searched for Pascal and found him sitting on the rail of Hook's ship. When had he gotten there?

"Pascal, why wasn't the cargo in the Leviathan's lair? It isn't going to bring that sort of stuff along, and what exactly is this cargo we're searching for? How am I going to know what it is when we do find it?"

Pascal clicked his tongue before jumping onto the main deck from his perch on the rail. "It is interesting that it wasn't in its den. Maybe it's floating in the sea of death out there, or perhaps someone has already claimed the prize." he shrugged. "It's your job to find it, little dove, not mine. And as far as the other thing." he brought a finger to his lips. "It's a secret that only the king can tell you."

"The king?" Hook asked as he approached and narrowed his eyes on the wizard. "Pascal."

Pascal's smile brightened. "Good to see you, Hook, and yes, Arie here was sent by the king to retrieve something for him. I also know why you're here."

Hook's eyes widened, and I could have sworn his skin paled for a second. He cleared his throat and said, "Yeah, looks like we both have bounties from the king."

So that's why he was here. King Roland had given us both the same job, but why? Was he that desperate for some stupid cargo that he was handing out orders to anyone? If this was coming from the king, it was more likely that he had something of Hook's, or someone.

"Sir, we're retaining too much water and these masts are shot."

I could hear it then, the soft creak of the boards beneath us, the way the ship tilted slightly. It was time to abandon ship. *The Marauder* wouldn't last much longer.

I sighed, knowing what I'd have to do next. As appealing as it sounded, I couldn't leave Hook and his men to fend for themselves. Not in Scarlett's Lagoon anyway. Plus, having someone else on board the *Betty* who knew about the Leviathan, who had lived through its attack could be beneficial. But why in hells did it have to be Hook? I'd have welcomed any other rival ship, maybe with a little less hostility, than him. We'd been at each other's throats for years. I still wasn't over the bounty he'd stolen from me. A hydra, one so massive that I would have had to place its head on the bowsprit of the *Betty*.

If he even agreed to it, what message would that send to my crew? It was one thing to save him, but it was entirely different to allow them aboard. What would they think?

I was so lost in thought that I hadn't realized Keenan spoke to me until he tugged on my sleeve, pulling me to the side.

"Arie, are you listening to me?"

"Sorry, Kay, what's up?"

"Hook knows more about the Leviathan than anyone. We are after the same thing; don't you think it would be beneficial to have him on board?"

Keenan was a smart man, he'd come to the same conclusion, but I wasn't ready to admit that yet. "Aren't there enough broody men on the *Betty* already?"

"Captain, this may be our only shot. We don't know where it is, and what happens if Hook finds it first? Wouldn't it be better for him to lead us there so you could ensure you were the one to kill it?"

Again, always the logical one. A smirk rose to my face. "How are you always so insightful?"

Keenan smiled back, much warmer than my own, and shrugged.

I sighed, already regretting what I was about to do.

Around us, Hook's ship was in shambles. Most of his crew had either fallen to the depths or died defending the ship. The half that remained weren't in the best of shape, and they all waited for their captain to speak. Hook kept his back to them, gazing out to the open sea.

"Why don't you and what's left of your crew come with us back to Vallarta," I hadn't planned on going to Vallarta, but we needed supplies and hopefully someone who could point us in the right direction. It was the only smart choice.

Hook craned his neck, his eyes void of emotion. "I would rather jump into the sea of sirens before getting on that." He nodded toward my ship.

I wasn't quite ready to admit that I needed his help, so I settled on something that might pique his interest more. "Do you want to get out of the Leviathan's territory, or not?"

Smith clasped Hook's shoulder. "There's no way *The Marauder* is making it out of this, captain. If we don't get off soon, we'll go down with her."

"A captain doesn't abandon his ship." He spoke through gritted teeth.

"A smart captain would," I said.

"You'd abandon the *Betty*?"

He was right, abandoning my ship was like abandoning the life I'd created for myself. I wasn't sure I could do it if the roles were reversed, but right now it didn't matter. We needed to get the hells out of here. "So, you'd abandon the few of your men that are still alive instead?"

We stood in silence for so long I almost gave up waiting for him to answer. I waved a hand at him and turned away.

"You better have ale aboard," he grumbled.

I whirled around and placed a hand at my chest. "Am I not a pirate?"

"And I get a cabin for myself." Hook pushed past me, grabbing one of the ropes and swinging himself over to the *Betty*.

"Is he always this broody?"

Smith shrugged. "You get used to it."

"That's highly unlikely."

Thankfully, I wouldn't have to get used to it. The second we reached Vallarta, we would go our separate ways. The quicker I got Captain Hook off my ship, the better.

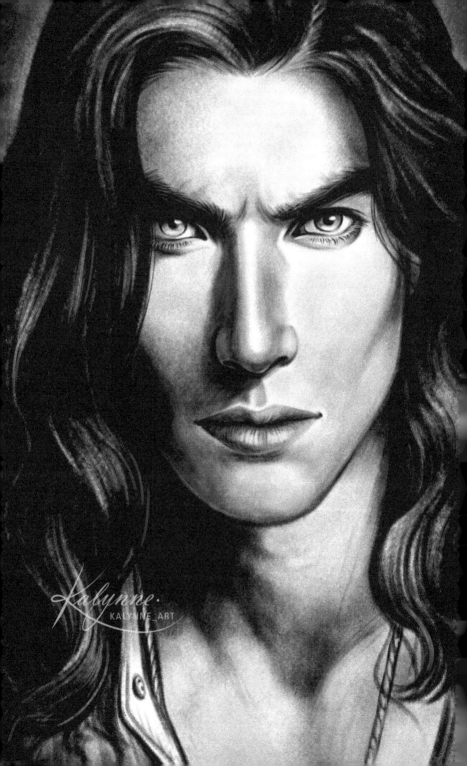

V. A PIRATE'S GAMBLE

LOSING A SHIP WAS AKIN TO LOSING YOUR SOUL, THE thing that made you a captain. Being forced to abandon your home would scar any pirate, but for Hook, it did more than that.

He sulked around the *Betty* for days, a bottle of rum in one hand and whiskey in the crook of his hook. His men had to carry him to bed most nights.

It was pathetic and at the same time, I found myself feeling sorry for him. Our roles could have been reversed… After all, the sirens had been looking for me. What if they'd found me first? They said they had come for me, but would they have spared my men? Being a captain, I found myself constantly worrying about my crew. Witnessing Hook's loss made my stomach whirl.

Why did it seem that at every turn, death followed us? The worst part was that there would be much more on the journey ahead. I could sense it in the air like an aroma, pulling me toward... something. It had started the second we sailed into Scarlett's Lagoon and its feeling of wrongness only worsened with time.

There were so many unanswered questions. Who was this woman who searched for me? Where had the Leviathan gone? Was I the reason Hook no longer had a ship? My pulse raced, the blood pounding in my ears making my head spin. I needed answers, and there was one person who'd give them to me. An old friend I hadn't seen in quite some time.

Sometime later, I sat crossed legged on a wooden barrel, staring down a royal flush like it was a warm plate of bacon. Well, on the inside anyway, on the outside I kept my face straight, unwavering as my opponents looked me up and down.

"She's bluffing." Nathaniel narrowed his eyes and I fought the urge to laugh. He wasn't much of a poker player, but he was one hell of a pirate. I'd met him while on a hunt for a Hydra. I was in over my head, almost lost until he showed up. I've never seen a grown man rip out a monster's heart before, but he had. Though, neither of us knew that the Hydra in question was cursed. It had settled into Nathaniel so fast that if it weren't for my knowledge of curses and poisons, he'd have died a slow and painful death. When he was well, I offered him a place on my ship, and he never looked back.

"Even if she is, I fold." Hector threw his cards face down and washed down his loss with alcohol.

We'd been at it for hours, and my pile of doubloons was growing rapidly. Hector, who mumbled irritants under his breath, had just enough to play one more round. Whereas Nathaniel continued to get harder and harder to fool.

As he tapped the table to check, the door opened, and Hook entered. My heart skipped. He looked better than he had this morning. His hair was combed and face washed. He'd even changed into clothes that Keenan had provided.

Smith decided he had been sulking long enough and sent him away from the alcohol and put him to work. It was amazing watching a small-stout man like Smith boss around someone as large and broody as Hook.

The captain wore a white linen shirt that clung to hard muscle, the sleeves rolled up to his elbows exposing the ink on his arm. I couldn't quite make it out from where I sat. I may dislike the man, but there was no denying the flutters in my stomach or the way my gaze refused to look anywhere besides him. My cheeks warmed and I sipped from my mug, hoping no one noticed.

Tonight, he seemed to be sober and no longer on the verge of death. I still didn't want to be anywhere near him. He'd been giving me the cold shoulder and refusing to say anything. When I mentioned the idea of working together, as much as it pained me to do so, he'd laughed in my face and said I was just as mad as the beast I hunted.

Rather than allow him to ruin this otherwise perfect evening, or cause my heart to flutter again, I scooped up my winnings and stood.

"Leaving so soon? And here I thought you'd like an actual

challenge." Hook beamed.

"Come again?" Hector scowled at him.

"Arie, you can't leave now, I was just about to win!" Nathaniel leaned back in his chair, a smug look on his face. Just because I was leaving, didn't mean I was admitting defeat. That look in his eyes begged to differ.

"I can, and I am. I'd rather not be anywhere near this one." I gestured to Hook before stalking toward the door.

"Are you sure you don't want to stay?" Hook slid into an empty chair and crossed his arms over his chest, the sleeves of his shirt tugging around every inch of the muscle in his arms. "I can make it worth your while. How about a little wager?"

My hand hovered over the door handle. If I walked out of this room, word would spread that I turned down a chance to beat Hook at cards. I'd never be able to show my face in the Ugly Duckling again. I sighed, returning to my chair.

"It had better be a worthy wager."

"If you win, you can ask me whatever questions you've been wanting answers to."

Well, this just got interesting.

"*Any* questions, and you have to answer them?"

He nodded. "But if I win, then I get to be the one to ask. And you'll get a chance to take more doubloons from me."

This was perfect. An easy win and a shot at answers. Looks like I was about to have a good night after all. I'd be able to figure out more about what brought him here. What did the king have on him that had him scurrying off to Scarlett's Lagoon? Why would he want to return to such a place, or what was his plan now his ship was gone? If he was after the Leviathan, how was he planning on going after it now? He sure as hells wasn't staying on this ship.

"Deal." I turned toward Hector and Nathaniel. Hoping they would take the hint that I wanted them to leave. Whatever questions I had, I wanted to do it without prying eyes and eavesdropping ears. They both looked between Hook and I, clearly not knowing what to say. Hector fidgeted with the little bit of winnings he had left, and Nathaniel crossed his arms to match Hook.

"Nathaniel," I said wearily.

Nathaniel kept his eyes glued to Hook as he stood and trailed behind Hector who kept glancing back at me. I wanted to laugh at their attempts to seem like big, protective brothers, but with Hook in the room it didn't feel right. He may be on my ship, but that didn't mean he'd get the privilege of knowing what my relationship was like with my crew. I had to keep up as much mystery as possible. Hopefully the questions he asked were ones that could be skirted. What was I saying? He wouldn't get the chance to win. Not with me as his opponent.

"Pirate rules, or boring regular person rules?" asked Hook.

"I'll say it again, are we not pirates?" I took a bottle of rum and set it in front of him.

Hook pulled out a cloth pouch and pulled on the drawstring, letting it open to reveal its contents: doubloons and lots of them. "Let's play." As I shuffled the cards, Hook poured us each a drink.

"You do know the house always wins right?" I said.

Hook set my drink down next to me before taking a long drink of his. His Adam's apple bobbed with each swig, and I found myself staring again.

"Not unless *I* take the house," Hook rumbled back.

Not a chance.

In poker, you never played the hand. You played the man across from you, and I was planning on doing just that. I dealt out the cards, placing three in the middle of the table face up: the queen of hearts, the two of spades, and last, the six of hearts. I waited as Hook threw some coins into the middle, making his first bet.

The key was to always watch for subtle hints. A raise of a brow or a wipe of one's nose; every movement made was one that could give away what kind of hand your opponent had. I'd learned through the years to use that to my advantage. Hook's face, however, was like a solid brick wall, impenetrable to most forces, but I too was a force to be reckoned with.

I surveyed my cards—pocket aces. Already my luck was shining through, and I matched his bet, tossing more doubloons into the pot. I decided to start off slow, knowing that if I pushed too hard, too fast, he'd realize what I was doing. While my hand was good, the best tactic when it came to cards was the bluff. Working a bluff to your advantage was not only important but crucial and, in this game, it was everything.

Never having played against Hook before, I'd have to maintain composure. There was no telling what he had in his own hand, and if I played my cards right, maybe I could get him to fold before this got much further.

Hook's gaze lifted from his cards to meet mine. It was interesting watching him play with one hand, but he did so flawlessly. I watched as he held the cards in his good hand and used his hook to toss coins into the middle. The coins just stuck to it, like it was magnetic. I didn't know how he did it, but I wasn't about to ask just then. Maybe it would be a good starter question for when I beat him.

Without so much as a blink in his direction, I picked up a card from the stack and placed it on the table—an ace of hearts. My heart nearly lodged itself in my throat, but my face stayed cool. Not daring to make a move other than to glance at my cards once more.

"Check," Hook said. I peered up at him to gauge his reaction, but his face was as stoic as ever. "Looking for something?"

Rather than answering, I tossed a few doubloons into the pot. I decided to play it safe and started with a small bet. "I'll raise."

Hook narrowed his eyes, tilting his head slightly as he considered me before throwing a stack into the pot. "I'll see your raise and raise you five more."

"Are you sure you want to lose your money this way, Hook? It would be pretty humiliating to lose to not only your rival, but a woman at that." I couldn't help myself. The desire to ruffle the feathers was all encompassing. It was how I played, a few bits of banter, the need to make my opponents second guess their hand.

"It won't be me who's humiliated," he clapped back.

I matched his raise, and with no more bets made, I laid down the final card; the river and a ten of hearts. Useless to me, but a possible gold mine to Hook—if he had the right cards.

"When I win, I'll expect your answers to be without deception. No skirting," I said, hoping a bit of banter would keep my nerves from rising more than they already were. The desire to ask questions was growing more and more the longer this game went on. I didn't trust him as far as I could throw him and right now my suspicions were that something was up.

"The only way you're winning this is if I let you, and I can assure you, I won't." Hook twirled a coin between his knuckles before tossing it into the middle, along with a small stack of others. "I can keep this up all night."

I bet he could.

Ugh. What was wrong with me? He was trying to rattle me, get under my skin so I'd fold and make it easy on him. Not a fucking chance.

I had three aces. The odds he had anything better weren't *that* great. But what if I was wrong?

I froze. If he won, he could ask me anything. He already knew why I was in Scarlett's Lagoon, so what else could he possibly want to know? Maybe he wanted to know about my powers, or what my secret was when it came to getting through a storm unscathed. All things that I wanted to keep a secret. I swallowed, hoping like hells he didn't win this. Why didn't I think this through?

"Just shut up and play," I said and knocked on the table, swallowing down the last of my drink. As I poured another, knowing I should probably slow down if I wanted to keep my wits, but it would ease my nerves.

Hook looked at me for a minute, threw back his own and slid his empty mug toward me. He was stalling, but why? Rolling my eyes, I poured the last bit of the bottle into his mug and slid it back. It was time to get this over with.

"Ladies first." He gestured toward me with his hook.

A grin crept to my face; he didn't have anything. If he'd had cards worthy of a win, he'd already be rubbing it in my face, throwing the cards at me as well as all his questions. Relief began to rise in my chest as I flipped over my cards, laying both aces in the middle of the table. "Three of a kind."

Hook frowned, his brow furrowing more than I'd ever seen and, in that moment, I knew I'd been victorious. I let out the breath I'd been holding and took a long hard drink, letting the liquid's warmth settle within me as I gathered the questions I was going to ask him.

"You call that a hand?" Hook *laughed*.

"A hand that has obviously bested..."

Hook tossed his cards right-side up to reveal his hand and I cursed. A flush. All hearts and a better hand than I had with my aces. My jaw dropped slightly as my victory turned to defeat and all joy was washed down by the fact that I'd lost.

Hook threw his head back and let out a throaty laugh. "You should see the look on your face. I didn't think you could get any paler!"

My stomach twisted into knots, unable to move or speak as I stared at the cards. I'd lost. His cards laid on the table, as if they were staring me down, taunting me until I couldn't breathe. I blinked hard, once then twice, but nothing changed. His cards were still the same.

"Shall we get right to it then?" Hook asked.

Every part of me wanted to refuse, to tell him that this was *my* ship, and I didn't have to abide by this stupid game. It was just that—a game. I sighed. I couldn't do that. He'd won fair and square, besting me at a game I was known to be victorious at. I slumped in my chair, finishing off another drink. "I'm going to need more of this if we're going to start with questions."

Hook's smug look was enough to make me want to hurl the empty bottle next to me at his face. I should have never allowed him to weasel his way into the game. I was the captain here, not him. So why did I take his bait? Because I actually thought I would win.

"First question, what does the king have on you? I noticed all of your crew is here, or at least the important ones from what I can tell."

"Something valuable. Next question."

Hook *tsked*. "No skirting, Arie. Tell me what the king has on you that would make you of all people do his bidding."

Honestly, I was surprised he didn't already know. I figured word would have spread far and wide by now that the king had my sister in his crummy hands waiting for me to make a wrong move so he could strike. "My sister," I mumbled.

Hook placed his hand behind his ear. "I'm sorry, what was that? You'll have to speak up."

"My *sister*. Someone I thought I'd hidden well. Apparently the king has more resources than I imagined."

I clamped my mouth shut. *Keep your answers simple, Arie.* The less he knew, the better.

Hook's lips pursed; eyes narrowed as he ran a hand along his beard. "Sister, huh? What exactly does he want you to do in exchange for her life?"

Wasn't that obvious? I wouldn't sail through Scarlett's Lagoon for shits and giggles. Plus, didn't King Roland ask him to do the same thing? "Why ask a question you already know?"

"Answer the question, Arie."

My hands balled into fists, my nails digging into my skin. I wished he would stop saying my name and forget he ever knew it. Him saying it made not only my skin crawl, but my stomach clench. I needed to get out of here.

"He wants me to retrieve some cargo, and before you ask, no, I don't know what that cargo is."

Hook nodded. "Your sister, how come no one has seen her or even knows who she is? I'd figure an orphan would want to keep the only family she has left at her side. Are you ashamed?"

I slammed my fist on the table sending cards flying in the quake of my fury. "I swear to Davy Jones himself, Hook, you better watch yourself. Just because I agreed to answer your questions doesn't mean I won't gut you where you sit." He was skirting a fine line and if he crossed it, I'd have Slayer show him what life would be like with two hooks for hands.

Hook held up his hand. "Then let me ask you this, if you fail to retrieve your cargo, how do you expect to get your sister free?"

Hells, why were these the questions he wanted answers to? What did he gain by this? Shouldn't he be asking where I kept my treasure, or ask me if I had the heads of my monsters in my quarters? Maybe he was trying to rile me up. Whatever it was I didn't like it and I was getting closer to the edge. My power rose to the surface, dancing along the edge of my consciousness. It was ready to be unleashed if necessary, and I only held it back by sure will.

"I'll find a way, I always do. Are we done here?"

"Not quite, I have one more question."

I stilled. Hoping to the gods he wasn't about to ask me anything related to my gift.

"Your fathers' deaths, some say *you* were the one to do it. That they were holding you back and you needed their freedom. Which I can say sounds like something a bloodthirsty pirate would do. Of course, you weren't a pirate then, but if you're anything like me…"

Hook trailed off, his words leaving me as once again I found myself unable to breathe. I drew Slayer from where it sat on the table and leapt, seeing nothing but red as I shoved him. The chair beneath him broke as we crashed to the floor. Before he could make a move, I pointed Slayer at his throat. How fucking dare he say such a thing.

"Don't ever mention them again," I said through gritted teeth. "I don't care that your men are on this ship. I *will* kill you and not blink."

Hook's eyes widened, frozen to the floor as I straddled over him. If it weren't for the fact that I wanted to get to Vallarta without bloodshed, I would have slit his throat and not give a damn about the consequences.

"Shit. Okay, all right. I didn't think—"

"No, you didn't." As I stood, I realized I was panting, unable to control my breathing or the tears that started to spill. More from my own rage and hurt than from sadness. I'd done everything in my power to do what was right, to honor both Malakai and Viktor. And this man had the audacity to say such things? I didn't need this.

"I crossed a line. I see that now." Hook held up his hands and shook his head. "I didn't mean to cause you pain. Not like this, anyway."

Dropping Slayer to my side, I wiped away the tears with the sleeve of my shirt and turned away from him. Unsure of how I'd allowed him to get to me like this, I was a captain for hells sake. The last thing I needed was for him to think of me as weak. My control was better than that, but too much to drink and a pirate who got under your skin would do that.

"Would it help if I shared something with you?" He didn't wait for an answer, simply grabbed the bottle with the most alcohol left and motioned for me to follow him outside. My hands shook with rage that still coursed through me. He obviously wanted me to follow, but I wasn't a dog to simply trail after him like a good girl. He really expected me to just get over the fact that he'd accused me of killing my fathers?

"Unless you don't want to ask your own questions?"

What? That wasn't part of the bet. Why would he do that? I should have left, just gone back to my quarters and ended the night. Instead, I followed after him.

Curse the gods, what was I doing?

Outside, the sun had finally set, leaving behind a sky cluttered with bright stars. A cool breeze whistled over the open bottle in my hand as I followed him toward the ship's rail. The sea was calm tonight, nothing but soft ripples that pushed us further to our destination.

Hook leaned over the side, resting his arms against the railing, and pulled out a silver locket. The chain dangled over his palm as he unclasped the two pieces. It sprung open, revealing a single painting. A small child with a huge, infectious smile that lit up his brown eyes. He looked so much like Hook that I could have mistaken it for him, down to the very same dimple.

"This is my brother, Clayton. He's much older now, but it's all I have of him."

I didn't know what to say, or what to do for that matter. I wasn't exactly sure how I'd expect this conversation to go, but this was far from it. He didn't need to tell me this. I'd lost the game, I answered his questions and we were done here. Then why was I buzzing with the need to hear what he had to say?

We stood in silence for a while before he cleared his throat. "We don't exactly see eye to eye. He's everything I'm not."

He said that last part so quietly, I would have missed it had we not been standing so close. "Where is he now?"

Hook clenched his fist until the knuckles turned white. His brows furrowed as he turned away from me. "He wanted to prove to me that I didn't have to live the pirate life anymore, that we didn't have to be *lost* anymore. He wanted to stay in Khan, but..." He looked back at me then, his eyes sorrowful. "Khan isn't *my* home. It never will be. He still wanted to prove to me that we could be more. So, he joined the king's army."

"King Roland's army?" I asked, more in disbelief than an actual question. If Hook claimed his brother was a good man, why in sea's sake would he join Roland's army. Surely there were better ways to prove his point.

"I begged him not to, but he was determined, and once Clayton set his sights on something, there is nothing that can stop him. When he told me this he had already joined, but what he didn't know was that King Roland knew exactly who Clay was."

Of course, he did. King Roland had resources, after all he'd managed to find Frankie and I'd done a damn good job at hiding her. Well… I thought I had. And, on the other hand, I believed it was really Pascal who carried the weight behind the king's power.

"Clayton never told me what happened, but he owes the king a lot of money and was supposed to kill the Leviathan and collect his cargo as payment. However, the fleet Roland sent wasn't enough. Clayton and a few others were the only survivors. I'm not sure how a sea monster could steal his precious cargo, but he's willing to do whatever it takes to get it back."

My chest tightened as Frankie flashed before my eyes. Waiting at the docks for me day after day. Hoping her big sister would come to take her away so they could be together again. Then finally taking matters into her own hands and searching for me. It was never my intention to leave Frankie for good. I just wanted to find the one responsible for killing our fathers. I was going to have to prove to her, prove to myself, that I would never abandon her again.

"The king has him, too?"

Hook nodded, and the twist in my stomach worsened. "Locked up like some… *fucking* animal. Said I have a choice, either watch my brother die a slow painful death, or retrieve what was taken from him."

Fire lit in Hook's eyes; his jaw clenched as rage burrowed into his words. "That's why *I* have to be the one to find the Leviathan. Clayton is a good man, a pure soul who is meant to live a long happy life. He shouldn't be sitting behind bars because his brother is a no-good-thieving pirate. So, when it comes down to it, I'll be collecting my bounty at any cost."

I understood the burning desire to save the one you care for. The same unrelenting need to take down everything in your path until you did so. Frankie's freedom was all I cared about right now. If I must slay the death beast and steal some stupid treasure, I would, and no one would stop me. It felt weird, wanting to comfort Hook, but our separate missions were lining up and I didn't know how to feel about any of this.

"There's one thing I just… I don't understand." He stepped back from the rail, turning to face me. "The entire island reeked of magic. Whatever happened there had been well before either of us showed up. I don't know what, all I know is that it smelled like…"

He paused, tilting his head to glance up at me before turning back to the water.

He could smell magic? I didn't know one could smell such things.

"Like what?"

"You."

Me? I certainly hadn't ever been there before, hadn't even used my magic until stepping on the island. There was no way my magic would linger like that. It had been potent around the island, thick in the air as we searched for the Leviathan, but all I smelled was the trees and the sea.

"Wait, how do you know what my magic smells like, or magic in general? Better yet, how do you know about *my* magic?"

Hook pursed his lips. "You're not the first witch I've encountered in my life, and sea witches are all the same. Thirsty for power, hungry for death. You seem to be just like the rest of them. So, tell me, why did the island smell like you?"

"What are you trying to get at? If you actually think I had anything to do with this you're out of your damn mind!" I jabbed a finger into his chest, pain trickling through it as it met solid muscle.

Hook slapped my hand away. "You have a lot of nerve—"

"And a lot of sassiness in her, don't you think so, Hook?"

I whirled around to find Pascal perched on a barrel a few feet behind us. His feet dangled, hitting against the wood, while his hands folded in his lap. "I like my women to have a little spunk."

"What do you want, Pascal?" I squirmed at his words. How long had he been there? Better yet, how did I not notice? I glanced at the bottle still clutched in my hand and shook my head. I *really* should have just gone to bed.

"Well, at first I was curious what our next step was, but this show of 'who's the better captain' is much more entertaining." Pascal jumped down from the barrel, his green tunic fluttering in the wind.

Hook kept still, his eyes fixed on Pascal, and I wondered what kind of past these two had. Another question for another time. Right now, I was done dealing with these two.

"I'm going to bed." I waved before setting off away from Hook and Pascal.

"Of course, little dove," he called after me. "Sleep tight, don't let the monsters bite!"

VI. THE UGLY DUCKLING

HOME.

I'd traveled far and wide in my time as a captain, but there was nothing that felt more serene than stepping on familiar soil. Vallarta bustled with pirates, townsfolk, and laborers as we made our way from the docks. Thankfully, all the vessels were ones that I didn't know, and we hadn't spotted any familiar faces… yet. I was hoping to keep this trip as fast and as low key as possible. After last night's two-person drinking party with Hook, and the bottle of wine I'd fallen asleep with, my head was pounding. I took it as punishment for allowing myself to open up to the one I was supposed to be rivaled with. It was a wonder how we'd made it here without tearing each other limb from limb. At least now I was finally going to get rid of him.

After he told me that the island had smelled of magic similar to my own, I'd spent the better half of the night tossing and turning. It just didn't make any sense. The Leviathan was a beast, a monster of the sea who terrorized ships and killed anyone in its path. Between the skulls that lined the cavern walls, and the smell of… me, nothing about this was adding up. Which was why I needed to speak with Hank—owner of the Ugly Duckling. If there was anyone who had the insight on where to go next, it would be him.

"Hector, Nathaniel, why don't the two of you head to the market. Get whatever's needed and tell Claire to put it on my tab. Make sure to give her my gift and my love."

Claire was what you'd call a businesswoman with a knack for trading goods and stealing hearts. She took care of all the ships that docked in Vallarta and had, occasionally, warmed my bed when I came for a visit. This time, however, she'd have to do with the handful of jewels I'd found a few months back.

"The rest of you, we aren't here for a stay. You have the day and then I want you all back on the ship by dusk." I turned away and nearly ran into Hook whose arms were folded over his chest. My eyes wandered, trailing over the intricate, thick muscle along his exposed arms. My face flushed when I realized I was staring, and heat rose between my legs.

Why does he affect me like this? I was supposed to hate him. I *did* hate him. This was simply a reaction from a sexually deprived female, nothing more. I needed to find a release, and soon—if only there was enough time.

I cleared my throat, biting my tongue as I stifled my arousal. "Do you mind?"

I was surprised to see him anywhere near me. I figured the second we stepped in Vallarta he'd be gone, and I wouldn't have to deal with his insufferable ass.

"I'm coming with you."

"The hell you are. We're in Vallarta, which means we don't have to be in each other's presence anymore."

He didn't budge, not even the slightest twitch as his eyes bore into mine. "You and I both know that you have a better chance at finding and killing that thing with me on the *Betty*. I've seen this thing up close and personal. Or did you forget?"

Who could forget when it was all anyone talked about any time we stepped foot in Vallarta for a solid year? Either way, having to spend more time with Hook was not something I wanted to do. His mimicking of Keenan's words had me cursing under my breath. I was absolutely going to regret this.

"You can come to the pub with me, and maybe if you behave, I'll consider it."

"Oh, I hope we're not behaving." Pascal purred from behind and I cringed. "It's more exciting that way."

"*You* can stay on the ship." I pointed toward the docks.

Pascal clicked his tongue. "And miss all the fun?"

I rolled my eyes, ignoring him as I turned toward my destination. I didn't have the time to waste on them.

The three of us walked side by side through Vallarta's market district. Waves of heat wrapped itself around me. Sweat dripped from my brow and a part of me wanted to summon clouds to shield from the sun. In town, the trees were sparse which left only the rows of buildings for shade. Even then, the breeze rolling off the sea gave little reprieve from the summer's heat.

We weaved in and out of the crowd, something that seemed to bother Hook more than myself. He kept his hook on the hilt of his sword and his hand curled in a fist, ready to strike whatever he deemed necessary. Vallarta was a place made for the glory of the common criminal to dwell. If anything, we were safer here than we were anywhere else. So, I wasn't sure what had made him so uptight.

Taking in a deep breath, my nostrils filled with the smell of food. From savory to sweet, the wafting smells made me miss my fathers and sister. It had been a long time since I had enjoyed a good home cooked meal. Maybe once this was all over I could do just that.

Several tents sat in rows along the dirt road, I could hear the distant clink of coin being passed from one hand to the other and the clank of metal on metal as weapons were crafted. We walked past a large table with smoke billowing from behind it like a serpent. If I weren't on a mission I would have stopped and spent more coin than I should on whatever delectable they were selling.

Just as we passed the last set of tents, a group of giggling children nearly ran us over as they shouted after one another. A smile tugged on my lips as I found myself relaxed for the first time in… *hells,* it had been a while since I truly felt like this.

Pascal, on the other hand, was attracting more attention than I would have liked. Every tent we passed he stopped to check out what they were selling. Most of the shop owners simply gave Pascal what he wanted just so he would leave. If it wasn't the scars on his face that scared them, his reputation would. The onlookers whispered behind their hands as we continued down the street. All of them backed as far from him as they could get.

"Maybe we should have insisted he stayed behind," Hook murmured so softly I barely heard him over the bustling crowd.

"As if he would have listened."

The tents began to dwindle as we traveled further from the market toward the darker part of Vallarta. Here, the streets were quiet save for the few people entering and exiting buildings. My eyes trailed upward to see a painted yellow duck on a wooden plank hung by a string on a post. The duck wore a tricorne style hat with a skull and crossbones. Below the duck the words 'Ugly Duckling' had been engraved. I pushed the door open and headed inside.

The familiar scent of wood smoke and ale hit me first, and my shoulders relaxed. Lanterns hung along the walls, giving off some light in the otherwise dark pub. Long wooden tables took up most of the floor, save for the open space where musicians tuned their instruments. Near the musicians, a small group sat around a circular table. Cards in hands, the players tossed coins into a rather large pot in the middle. I'd spent the better half of my time in Vallarta at that table learning how to fool others into thinking I was a formidable opponent. Really though, I just knew how to read people.

As we moved around tables, my earlier worries slowly dissipated leaving me with a sense of calm I hadn't felt in days. There was something about being in a room full of people who understood you and who fought the same battles you did, never having to worry about looking over your shoulder or wonder who was conspiring against you. At least, that's how it was in Hank's establishment. Everyone knew that if a single fight broke out in the Ugly Duckling, every person involved would meet Jerry—his rather scary meat cleaver.

He was the one who'd gifted me Slayer, a blade that had been his first. I'd met Hank a few days after my father's death. He'd been in town purchasing goods and I'd spent the better half of the day pleading, and offering a bit of coin, to let me accompany him to Vallarta. Frankie was already staying with our father's friends and I'd been itching to start my hunt. Ever since, he'd looked out for me, becoming somewhat of an uncle figure. He'd even helped me track down someone who could find a home for Frankie. I owed him everything.

"Arie!" A husky voice rang over the buzzing conversations. I found Hank slinging drinks, his grin growing. His long salt and pepper beard stretched down to his chest, and he'd combed wisps of hair over the top of his head. As if that would help. At my approach, soft wrinkles formed next to his green eyes.

"Hey, Hank."

"The usual?"

I nodded, settling into an open seat between a handsomely stout man and a petite woman who swayed back and forth with a drink in her hand. Hook and Pascal disappeared into the crowd and I sighed in relief, grateful to have a few moments to myself.

"What brings you back to Vallarta?" he asked, handing me a pint of rum.

The desire to spill my story sat on the tip of my tongue, and I swallowed it down with rum. I needed to speak with him, but it was going to have to wait until shift change. I didn't need prying ears to know what we were up to.

"Later?" I asked, and Hank nodded. "How's business?"

Hank shrugged. "I haven't had to bring Jerry out in almost a month. I don't know whether to be happy or disappointed."

I laughed and took another swig of my rum. Next to me, the woman bumped my arm as she sang some ballad with her glass raised above her head. "If you'd like, I can take him for a spin. I always wondered what it was like to use one."

"Slayer might get jealous." He winked and nodded to the dagger at my side.

"She's had her fair share of bloodshed."

"I don't doubt that for a second." Hank looked behind me. "Who are your friends?"

I turned to see Hook and Pascal standing behind me. Pascal pushed his way between me and the woman, extending his hand to Hank. "Pascal the Wizard, my dear sir."

Hank stepped back, nearly crashing into the bottles behind him, and snarled, "You brought the king's wizard in here?"

"I don't exactly have a say in the matter. It's something I'd like to discuss without the extra ears." I glanced around the room and then back to Hank who had turned a shade paler than he already was.

"Westly is in back, let me grab him and we can speak somewhere more private." Hank left, not taking his eyes off Pascal until he was beyond the door.

He returned a few minutes later and motioned for us to follow. Westly, Hank's teenage son, kept his eyes away from us. I caught a glimpse of his shaking hands before disappearing into the backroom.

Apparently, Pascal was known far and wide. I wasn't surprised, he frightened just about everyone he came across, but I suspected something more had happened here. I'd never seen Hank cower to anyone, not even Blackbeard.

"All right, what's going on?" Hank folded his arms over his chest, his eyes still pinned to the wizard as he pointed to him. "And why the fuck are you with *him*?"

"Didn't anyone tell you it's rude to point?" Pascal narrowed his eyes, his hands fidgeting at his side. I needed to change the subject, and fast.

Hook stepped closer to Pascal, his free hand resting near his sword. I nodded, thankful that he'd felt the same thing I did. We didn't need trouble, especially inside the Ugly Duckling.

I gave Hank the entire run down of what had happened over the last several days. From being captured, to the empty cave, not leaving out a single detail. Hook had chimed in a few times to give extra detail and by the end, Hank looked like he was going to be sick.

He'd taken a seat during my retelling, his hand playing with the length of his beard. Seconds passed before he moved. I didn't even see him pick up Jerry until he was charging toward us. Not us, Pascal.

"I'll kill you!"

"Whoa, Hank!" I jumped sideways, catching Hank's hand before Jerry could slice Pascal's head clean off. "As much as I would love to see the wizard bleed, he has to come out of this alive."

The rage in Hank's eyes simmered, but he kept Jerry above his head.

"Hank—"

"After today, if you so much as step foot in Vallarta, I won't hesitate to use this. No matter who tells me not to." Hank stalked back to his corner and slammed his cleaver on the table. His shoulders rose and fell with each breath. I knew the anger that swelled within him, I had the same reaction every time I thought of his part in my sister's capture. But to threaten Pascal? Had he completely lost his mind?

"Keep pointing that cleaver at me and see what happens. Or do you not remember our last encounter?" said Pascal.

Hank froze.

"What happened?" I asked.

"Not your concern. What can I do to help?" Hank turned to me.

"I need to find someone who might know where the Leviathan would go or know where to look. I know the monster is a mystery to most, but—"

"It's massive and deadly. It would leave a trail of sorts. We just need to know where to look." Hook interrupted. I'd forgotten he was still here. He'd stuck to the corner of the room and hadn't so much as made a single peep until then.

"Is there anyone that you know who might be able to help us?" I asked, pulling the attention back to the matter at hand. "I'm willing to pay."

Hank paced, mulling over his thoughts before speaking. "There's only one person I know who may be able to help, but Arie, he's not one to trifle with. I don't exactly trust him, but he, and those he works for now more than just about anyone. He may even still be here with Roxanne, one of the brothel owners."

"Who is he?" Hook asked.

"Trouble."

VII. BARGAINS AND BREWS

HANK LED US BACK INTO THE MAIN ROOM OF THE UGLY Duckling, which was much more crowded than when I'd first arrived. Patrons filled most tables, and the bar was overcrowded with drunken pirates. The noise level rose as music chimed through the room. Those who weren't dancing were stuck in deep conversations, most too busy to notice us as we walked by. All except the woman I'd sat next to, who was whispering into the ear of the man next to her. They looked up at us when we passed.

Hank stopped at the other end, just short of a small group of patrons. A single male sat surrounded by several women who looked like they'd come from the brothel. They all wore tight fitting corsets, long sleeveless dresses that exposed more skin than I ever dared to, and their busts were so squished together that it was a wonder how any of them were able to breathe. The one who sat on the far side of the table lifted her gaze to meet mine, her lips curled, and she leaned forward.

"Well, hello there, looking for some fun?" She winked, tossing her black curls behind her as she pursed her red lips. Golden bands wrapped around the bronze skin of her arms and I lost myself in the golden specks shimmering in her eyes. If it weren't for more pressing matters, I would have taken her up on the offer.

"Sorry, Roxy, she's here to speak with him." Hank nodded toward a man and women who were locked in each other's grasp as they attacked one another like hungry animals.

Roxy's face soured as she nudged the man next to her. "Jameson, this pretty little thing wants a word."

"I'll be at the bar if you need me," Hank whispered before leaving us.

"How about you, pretty boy, are you looking for some fun?" Roxy batted her eyes at Hook who cleared his throat.

"Maybe another time."

Pascal butted in, stepping past Hook to sit at the only empty chair. "Did someone say fun?" He rested his cheek on his hand, licking his lips. The entire table stilled, obviously they knew who sat before them. The woman opened her mouth to speak, when I grabbed him by his collar and yanked him up and out of the chair. I probably shouldn't have manhandled the scary wizard, but my patience was running thin.

"Down, boy." Shoving Pascal aside, I turned to Jameson who'd finally surfaced from the nape of a woman's neck.

"What do we have here?" The man Roxy called Jameson sat up in his chair, his light brown hair was unkempt, and lipstick traced along his cheek. His tattered shirt hung open, missing half of its buttons, and his chest glistened with sweat. He narrowed his dark eyes on me before letting out a huff. "You're Arie Lockwood."

Every one of the girls at the table stilled. Those who weren't already staring whirled around to gape at me. I'd spent many nights in this pub and not once did any of the patrons look at me like these ladies did. An unease washed over me, and it took all my strength to stay rooted where I was. People knew of me, my name had been a thing of chatter ever since becoming a hunter. This felt different. Their looks were softer, almost saddened.

Roxy's head shot up. "The one the king has been ranting about?"

The king was ranting about me. I shouldn't have been surprised; the man had put me on display in front of his peers and demanded I do as he said. As if I were some good little pup for him to order around. A lump formed in my throat as I thought of Frankie. What was he doing to her? Was she safe? I turned to Jameson. "I need information."

Already I knew this would come back to bite me. Asking for information was just as bad as asking for a favor, and being indebted to a stranger left a sour taste in my mouth. Especially one that came with a warning label from Hank. *Trouble*. What kind was I about to get myself in?

"What can I do for you?" Jameson purred, pushing the woman on his lap off as he leaned over the table.

"I'd prefer if we spoke in private."

Jameson shook his head. "If you want privacy, you came to the wrong man. As you can see." He pulled the woman back on his lap. She yelped and giggled as he nuzzled between her breasts. "I love when people watch."

Ugh. I pinched the bridge of my nose, my other hand begging to bring out Slayer. If he wanted to be the entertainment, I'd gladly show him a time he wouldn't forget. Sighing, I dropped both hands. I needed to get my point across without killing someone. The last thing I needed was to get blood all over Hank's floor.

"Maybe this will help move things along." Pascal opened his hand to reveal a small red diamond in his palm. It glistened against the low lighting of the pub. Where was he hiding that? Did he have more?

Beside me, Hook twitched, and he stuffed his hands in his pockets. His eyes widened at the diamond in Pascal's hand. A bead of sweat dripped down his face and it was like I could almost hear his thoughts. He wanted that just as much as I did, but maybe it could get us what we both wanted.

Jameson nearly shot out of his chair. He curled his hands around Pascal's open palm, his panicked eyes scanned the room. "Do you want to get us all killed? If one of these fools saw that—"

Pascal laughed. "Come now, dearie, you don't actually think a wizard of my power would allow just anyone to see this beauty?"

Jameson let go of Pascal's hand as if it stung him. His eyes narrowed on the wizard and a second later his brows rose. Yep, he knew exactly who sat at his table.

"Ladies, will you excuse us?" I said.

As the ladies left the table, Roxy folded her hands over her chest, not budging from her seat even as Jameson cleared his throat. She narrowed her eyes and her jaw clenched, unmoving as she stared him down. No one dared to speak as Roxy's fire seemed to only make Jameson happier. Already I found myself liking this girl. Jameson threw his head back and laughed. "Fine, all right. If you'd like to speak with me, Roxy will have to stay. She's not going to leave this alone, so I suggest we just get down to business, yes?"

I sat down in one of the vacant chairs, keeping an eye on Roxy as she refused to look anywhere but at me.

"We're looking for a way to track the Leviathan." No time to waste getting to the point. After all, night was approaching, and I needed to get back to the *Betty*.

"The beast of Scarlett's Lagoon? Why in seven hells would you want to track that thing?" Roxy shot out before Jameson could open his mouth.

"You'll have to excuse Roxy, she doesn't always remember her manners." Jameson bit back, glaring at Roxy in the process. Though only for a moment before shifting his gaze back to Pascal. Was that worry in his eyes? I didn't know this man, but I'd seen just about every person look at the wizard the same way. I wondered what kind of stories Jameson knew about Pascal.

"Can you tell us how to find the beast or not?" I hissed, already tired of this charade.

"No, but I can inquire with those who hold the power to do so." Jameson eyed me warily, but after a few moments of silence, stood and turned around to face an open window. He let out a soft whistle and seconds later a raven perched itself on the windowsill.

The bird was large, bigger than any I'd ever seen. Its wings spread nearly as long as the windowpane and its beady eye peered at me sending shivers down my back. Jameson ran a hand along its ebony feathers, clicking his tongue in odd manners until the bird turned its focus on him. As he spoke to it, the bird stilled, standing without a single flutter of its wings. As Jameson pulled away, the raven took one last look at me before taking flight to the east.

"What in the bloody *hells* was that?" asked Hook.

"Her name is Morrigan, and if I were you, I would refrain from staring next time." Jameson turned to look at me. "It will take a little bit for her to get back with your information, in the meantime, why don't you all have a drink and relax?"

Relax? I didn't have that kind of time, *Frankie* didn't have that kind of time.

"How long?" Hook spoke again; it was like he'd pulled the thoughts right from my mind. I was relieved he'd done so because I was still reeling over the raven. Those beady yellow eyes staring at me as if searching my soul for whatever it wanted to know.

"As long as it takes." Jameson stood, grabbing Roxy by the arm. She had fallen silent since the raven's arrival. "Now if you will excuse me. I have to take the girls back to the brothel. I'll be back soon with your information."

"It was nice to meet you, Arie. Maybe when you come back around you can stop into my establishment for a drink?" Roxy slid a hand over my shoulder before heading out the door.

At their departure, Hook spun and lifted his hook as if pointing an accusatory finger at me. "Do you really trust this guy? How do we know he's legit? Hells, how do we know he won't take off with the diamond?"

"Because I still have it." Pascal stood from his chair and tapped Hook on the shoulder. "So uptight and broody. Maybe you should have gone to the brothel with him."

Fire lit in Hook's eyes as Pascal swayed back and forth to the music, making his way toward Hank.

"Look, this is our best shot." I leaned back and rested my arm against the back of the chair. "Unless you have a better idea?"

The irritation in his face told me no, and a part of me was disappointed. Having to rely on the word of a man I just met wasn't exactly what I had in mind when we stopped in. My body writhed with that same irritation. The king wasn't going to give me all the time in the world, and I already used up a good portion of what limited time I had. Now we were wasting even more.

Angry *and* irritated, I waved a hand at Hook and made my way to where the alcohol awaited me. Hank had a full mug ready when I approached the bar.

"You get what you needed?"

"I'll find out soon enough." I shrugged. "Hey Hank, how well do you know this Jameson guy?"

"Well, he's a member of a guild. They're supposed to be on the up and up, but sometimes Jameson isn't exactly the most honorable of men. It's why the guild sends him to do more of the dirtier jobs. He isn't afraid to get his hands bloody."

Hank held up a hand. "I know what you're thinking, but trust me when I tell you he knows his stuff. His information is always good and as long as you're willing to pay his price, which is usually pretty steep, he'll come through."

It would have been nice to know before that we'd have to pay a hefty price for information. I also hadn't expected Pascal to come through like that.

Speaking of the wizard, I turned around to find him in a darkened corner speaking to some strange man. Hook was nearby, all his focus was on their conversation. *Good.* At least one of us was keeping an eye on him. He was more of a mystery than this Jameson guy.

What treasures could he produce out of thin air? When we left the king's castle, Pascal hadn't taken anything with him. Not a trunk with clothes, or a satchel with coins. Yet, he'd somehow managed to produce all of that without worry.

Just how strong was his magic?

"I never thought I'd see the day when Arie Lockwood and Hook would be in the same room as one another without swords drawn." The woman who'd been eyeing me up earlier stepped in front of me, blocking my view of both Hook and Pascal.

She didn't seem as tipsy as earlier, though her words slurred slightly. She towered over me, her arms nearly as big and round as Keenan's. Her blonde hair cascaded over large shoulders while her sun-kissed skin was covered in various inked designs. The blade on her hip was smaller than Slayer, and her fingers dangled over it as if waiting to make a move. Her ivory blouse and breeches clung to every curve while her black boots sported its own blade. I blinked, but they were still there. Two small blades protruding from the tips. I needed to get me a pair of those.

I took in a deep breath, the scent of salt and sea hit my nostrils like a battering ram and my nose wrinkled.

"Can I help you?" I asked.

"You can start by telling me what you're up to. If you and Hook have teamed up, I want to know why."

My brow rose. "Very bold of you to demand answers out of someone you don't even know." Who did this woman think she was? Demanding things like she was superior in some way. I didn't owe her anything besides a swift kick in whatever orifice was closest.

"Tell me what I want to know, *witch*, and no one needs to get hurt." She said *witch* as though it pained her to say it.

Fists clenched, I stood, forcing her to step back. "I suggest you take your friend here"—I nodded to the man behind her—"and find someone else to harass, because I promise you, you don't want to go there."

The woman threw her head back and laughed. "So scary, the big bad monster hunter thinks she can threaten us, Bobby."

Bobby's lips curled into a menacing grin. "This one needs to be taught some manners."

The woman took a step forward until she was inches from my face. "I'm a bounty hunter too, though the monsters *I* take down are deadlier than yours. So, you can either sit down and let me collect my bounty, or you can have the same fate as Hook."

A bounty hunter? Hook had a bounty on his head and didn't tell me? *Hells*, did he even know? And why in sea's sake didn't she just go after him instead of taunting me? As if she needed permission.

The king already had Clayton, so it wouldn't make sense for him to take out Hook like this. The man had many enemies, so it was possible that anyone could have placed one on him. If I weren't a better person, I would have left this woman to do her job and thought nothing more of it.

"I'm only going to ask this one more time. What are the two of you up to?"

"Didn't you know? We've gone and fallen in love and are meant to marry." I said as I gave the biggest fake smile I could muster.

"Think you're cheeky, huh? How about I cut that cute little face of yours up and see how funny you think this is then?" The bounty hunter narrowed her eyes. "Bobby, find Hook."

I dared a glance behind her to find Hook still listening in on Pascal. His shoulders tensed and brows furrowed, though the hardness of his eyes had finally started to soften in the time we'd been together. I may not have been able to stand the man, but I also wasn't about to sit idly by while he got attacked. There was still the issue of the Leviathan, and as much as it pained me to admit, he was going to come in handy when the time came to take the beast down.

"Sorry, Bobby, you'll have to go through me first."

"Through you?" The woman laughed again, this time she held her stomach as if pained. "That's not a problem."

Not giving the woman a chance to grab her blade, I smashed my glass over her hand and shoved her back. Shards of glass sprinkled over my arm and I winced as one sliced my hand. Blood trickled to the floor. So much for not spilling blood. *Sorry Hank.*

She wasn't much bigger than I, and bounty hunting wasn't for the weak. Then again, she was human as far as I could tell. This woman had no idea what she'd just gotten herself into. Bobby lunged forward, but I dodged. He ran into a stool, and I kicked him in the back, sending him crashing to the floor.

After that everything was a blur. The entire room turned into an all-out brawl. I ducked as a chair barreled toward me. It missed me by inches and crashed into dozens of bottles behind the bar. I winced.

If these two bounty hunters didn't kill me, Hank would.

"Arie, what did you do?" Hook panted as he threw a punch.

"*Me?* This one's after *you.*" I nodded to the woman who charged at me. This time her blade was drawn. Her eyes settled on mine, her brows knitting together as she charged. I drew Slayer and settled in for the dance. Where she jabbed, I countered with my own. I dodged her attack, slicing Slayer behind me as I rolled out of the way. She cried out, blood dripping down her leg.

Take that. A smile crept to my lips. I didn't always get the chance to have a showdown with humans, but when I did it brought out the fire in me.

The woman cursed, limping as she came at me once again. Something grabbed me from behind, holding my arms in place. I bucked and kicked to no avail.

"I've got her, Cecilia," Bobby shouted.

"Hold her still so I can gut her like a fish!" Cecilia's crazed eyes widened as she stalked closer. Anger lit her face like a flame.

This was not how my story was going to end. Without a second thought I threw my head back, cracking it against Bobby's face who wailed as he dropped me. I twirled and jabbed Slayer into Bobby's chest, he slumped to the ground, and behind me Cecilia cried out.

"You *bitch*. I'll kill you for this!"

"Arie," Hank shouted, "catch!"

I spun as he threw Jerry up in the air. I caught it just in time to connect with Cecilia's neck, severing her head in one final swoop. It rolled to the ground, blood splattering across my face as her body twitched before slumping to the floor. Her head sat at my feet, and an involuntary shiver crawled up my back. I hated killing unnecessarily, and while she'd been coming at me, I still preferred to only take down monsters.

"Unless you want a similar fate, I suggest you leave." Hank's voice thundered through the pub and those who'd been brawling halted. Each one took in the display of death before me and bolted through the door just as a familiar face walked in.

"Looks like I missed all the fun." Jameson stepped over groaning men as he approached. The raven from earlier perched on his shoulder.

Sighing, I fought the urge to slump to the ground right then and there. This journey was becoming much more than I bargained for, and all I wanted to do was sleep. My body ached and yet, now that Jameson was here, there was more work to be done. I just hoped he had good news.

VIII. Hidden Secrets

BROKEN GLASS, SPLINTERED WOOD, AND BLOOD littered the Ugly Duckling's floor. Cecilia and Bobby were taken care of, thanks to Pascal who'd worked some of his magic. All it took was a simple touch and their bodies disappeared.

Hank had refused my apologies, stating that it wasn't my fault even though I was the one who'd mouthed off to hunters. It just wasn't in me to back down, especially when they threatened people I cared… well, people.

I shot a look at Hook who had been helping Hank clean up. He'd taken off his shirt that was now torn and tattered, which left him barechested. His skin glistened with sweat and practically shimmered in the dim light. Every curve of his chest and stomach looked as if it were carved from a god. My eyes trailed upward, noticing that he'd pulled his hair into a bun. The faint dimple in his cheek appeared as he laughed at whatever Hank told him.

"Arie, are you listening?" Keenan asked. He'd shown up not long after the party, having heard some people at the docks talk about a brawl. "If you hold that mug any tighter, you're going to break it. I don't think Hank can afford any more broken glass."

Darting my gaze from Hook, I looked down at my white knuckled grip on the mug and shook my head. "Sorry, what were you saying?"

"Did she say who gave out the bounty?"

"No, though I plan to ask Hook that question once we leave."

Bounties were usually only given out by the wealthy or the royals. I'd already eliminated the possibility of Roland, though he wasn't the only king or queen in all the realms. Who knew how far Hook had traveled in his time as a pirate? The seven seas were vast and full of adventure and ships waiting to be boarded. For all I knew it could be a rival captain who'd felt the wrath of Hook and wanted payback.

Jameson approached from his talk with Pascal, throwing the diamond in the air and catching it as he took one of the unbroken chairs. The raven still perched on his shoulder. "Payment has been made, so are you ready to hear what I have to say?"

Maybe some good news would make me feel better about what had just happened.

"Get on with it, then," Hook grumbled, and I jumped, not realizing he'd stopped cleaning.

"My elder knows of your… predicament… and he has consulted

with the Oracle."

A lump formed in my throat, and I swallowed, my heart nearly jumping out of my chest as that name rolled off Jameson's tongue. "The Brotherhood's Oracle?"

The guild, also known as the Brotherhood, was a band of assassins who were meant to keep the Enchanted Realm safe. I knew very little about them, but what I did know was that their elders were some of the most influential and wealthy people in the world.

I froze. Could they have put the bounty on Hook? I shook my head; they would have done something like that internally. They wouldn't hire hunters, would they? I needed to talk to Hook about this. Soon.

"The one and only. Also, Morrigan says that there is something the brotherhood requests of you." Jameson held out a scroll, a green ribbon wrapped around it and tied in a bow.

Ignoring the fact that his bird could speak to him, I took the scroll and pulled on the ribbon and rolled it out.

Ms. Lockwood,

We, the Elders of the Brotherhood, would like to extend to you our gratitude for reaching out about your current problem. The Leviathan is a great threat to all, so we'd like to offer you a trade. The information you receive from Jameson in exchange for allowing him to accompany you on this journey. Jameson is a highly skilled hunter like yourself and can be a tremendous help.

Good luck.
-RH

An assassin on *Black Betty*? Death surrounded me enough as it was, having him on board would only make that worse. Why in sea's sake would they want him to accompany me, to ride into a likely death? Maybe this was just a way for them to get rid of him. And who was RH?

"Did you know they'd do this?" I asked Jameson.

"Unfortunately, I don't have a say in the matter."

So, neither of us wanted this. Fantastic. "Fine. Deal. But I'm in charge, got it? And if you cross me, or any of my crew? I will cut off those precious balls of yours and feed them to the Leviathan myself."

Jameson huffed. "Fine, but I get a room to myself."

I rolled my eyes. Were these men so insecure that they had to demand their own bedrooms? I wasn't about to cater to him. If he wanted a cabin to himself then he could sail his own damn ship.

"What else do you have to tell me?" I waved the parchment at him.

"That the Leviathan is not what you think." Jameson leaned forward and rested his arms on the table. "They believe it's much smarter and more calculated than other monsters. Some even think it's as intelligent as us humans. My elder said to be cautious when going up against it and to use the powers within to guide you. What that's supposed to mean, I don't know."

None of that was helpful. I'd already suspected that the Leviathan was smart. Rows and rows of skulls flashed through my mind.

"And the location of the Leviathan? The whole reason I came here…"

"According to the oracle, all you need to do is return home and all answers will be revealed." Jameson rolled his eyes. "Cryptic as ever. She really does like her mystery, isn't that right, Morrigan?"

The raven squawked before fluttering off and out the open window.

Home. I shivered as I dwelled on the thought of returning there. After that night my sister and I became orphans I swore to never return. My throat tightened. Curse the damned gods I didn't want to do this. My entire body broke out in a sweat. I fought to breathe, and my vision blurred. Everything started to go dark before a hand fell on my shoulder.

"Arie, are you okay?" My panic lessened as Hook's words lulled me back to a calm state. "Do I need to ask this man to leave?"

Jameson laughed. "As if you could–"

"I'm fine. Touch me again and we won't be." I bit out, even though his hand warmed something deep within me.

Hook threw his hands up. "Not even if my life depended on it."

The warmth faded and I instantly regretted snapping at him. What was wrong with me?

"Are the love birds at it again?" Pascal scooted closer to the group. He flipped his chair around so his chin could rest on the back.

Ignoring him, I swallowed, trying to wrap my brain around what I had to do. I hadn't stepped foot back home since that night. When Frankie and I left, I'd sworn to never return until the one responsible was taken care of. There were so many memories, too much pain and sorrow left in my heart that the mere mention of it sent me into a panic attack. The strong facade I carried was crumbling around me and I didn't know what to do.

Frankie was locked away, I was about to sail with a rival, a wizard, and an assassin with nowhere to go if one of them crossed me, and a cryptic message about intelligent monsters and having to relive my nightmares. I almost ran out of that room until Pascal spoke.

"There's been word from the king."

"And?" My stomach clenched, I knew our time was limited, but surely he couldn't expect results this fast, right?

"Patience, little dove." He smirked, took a drink, and cleared his throat before continuing. "We have a few extra days. If we do not bring the monster's head to him by then… well..." He looked at me and made a swiping motion across his neck with his thumb.

My sister. I had no choice. If we were going to find the monster and save innocent lives, I needed to go back. For Frankie I would have to suck up these inconveniences and find any means necessary to free her.

It was time to go home.

"How long has it been?" asked Hook.

"Eight. Eight *very* long years."

We'd set sail shortly after leaving the Ugly Duckling. The crew had yet again been displeased with another guest aboard the *Betty*, and some voiced their concerns, but overall Keenan managed to keep things under control.

Bellavier wasn't too far from Vallarta so it was only a day's travel.

I led the way toward the very place I swore to never return to. As my childhood home appeared through a clearing of trees, my heart thudded in my chest and blood pounded in my ears, I had to force myself to breathe.

The three-story home was exactly as I remembered. All except for grass that grew as tall as my knees and shattered windows that showed just how long I'd been away. The last time I was here my fathers were dead and I had taken Frankie and ran. We'd left with nothing but a small pack of belongings and no hope in our hearts. Panic rose in my chest and I fought the urge to curl up in the grass and weep.

The front door hung on broken hinges and when I pushed it open, it squeaked. I tried to ignore the men who followed me in, their eyes seeing the same destruction that I had once lived through. I bit my tongue, swallowing down the fear that threatened to overtake my mind.

Stay focused, Arie.

Now I was here, I realized I had no idea what I should be searching for. Everything my fathers had built was gone. What could still be here that would give me any idea about the location of a monster?

My eyes fell on the two stains in the wood floor by the fireplace. They'd since faded, but I could still make them out even after all this time. Visions of years past rushed forward. My fathers lifeless bodies lying together, their hands clasped in one another's.

I swallowed a sob and blinked away tears before giving orders.

"Everyone spread out, see what you can find. If you come across anything odd or of interest, holler for me."

We drew sticks to split up into three groups, one group per floor. Hook and Nathaniel took the upstairs, Hector and Pascal took the middle, while Keenan and I searched the basement.

I'd always hated it down here and to this day it gave me the chills. Though the cold draft that followed us down the stairs didn't help.

When we made it to the bottom, I clutched the makeshift torch I'd made and started looking for… something.

Boxes leaned against a wall, some of them labeled and others so covered with dust and mildew the words weren't legible. Though one box had my heart aching. I could only make out the F, but I knew its contents. Frankie and I each had a box of our belongings from when we first were adopted by Viktor and Malakai.

Blinking back more tears, I swore. Poor Frankie locked up and alone because of me. Damnations, why did I leave her? None of this would be happening.

I'm not giving up, Frankie. I will come for you.

I had to say it over and over for fear of not believing it myself. Everything felt entangled and messy, and I wished I knew what to do.

Across from the boxes was an old workbench fit with woodworking equipment and other tools now rusted and covered in dirt and dust. Next to that was a large bookcase filled with different trinkets and books. I'd always questioned why my Malakai had decided to keep it down here. To me, it deserved a place where it could be seen by more than just him.

Keenan stood next to it, examining a wooden doll Viktor had carved for my sister. The eyes were still missing and one of the legs was only halfway carved, but I remembered how long he had worked on it. My gut wrenched once more, and I brought my gaze back to the books along the middle shelf. One, in particular, stuck out to me, a green leather spine with golden symbols that looked nothing like any language I'd ever seen.

"Keenan, what do you make of this?" I asked, grabbing the book from the shelf.

Before he could answer, the floor beneath our feet shook and the bookcase opened inwards to reveal a small, dark hole. Large enough for someone to crawl through.

"Did you know that was there?"

I shook my head and rubbed my face. I'd lived here my entire life and never knew. I marveled at the thought that this could have been the best hide-and-seek spot in existence.

Keenan knelt and peered up at me. "Shall we?"

We had to duck to fit through. Darkness surrounded us. Keenan lit a candle he had grabbed from the bookshelf and held it up. Soft light barely illuminated the small room, but what we could see made my mouth drop open. Silk drapery hung like waves along with the ceiling and then cascaded down the walls to meet at hardwood floors that looked like timber from the oak trees that grew behind the house. I fought the desire to run my hands through the fabric and instead shifted so I could take in the rest of the room. Keenan walked toward the middle where candles covered a table. As he lit each one, the room grew brighter to reveal seashells in various sizes hanging along the walls, each casting an array of dancing light along the floor. Something in me woke, as if my soul had come alive.

All my worries and troubles dissipated, as something else settled in its wake. I couldn't put a finger on what it was, but it was almost euphoric.

Along the far wall stretched a mirror that reflected the light even more than the seashells did. My reflection shimmered in the mirror, wavy red locks flowing as though I were underwater. Green eyes stared back at me, almost like I was seeing them for the first time. My breath caught in my throat as I looked down and saw, not a set of legs, but a luminescent tail coated in greens and blues. Instead of feet, a fin swayed back and forth. My legs buckled, and I landed hard on the wood floor, but nothing mattered just then. Nothing but me and my reflection. I had no idea what this meant, was this a mind trick? Someone was toying with me. Yet somehow this *felt* right—tail and all.

"D-do you see this, Kay?" I asked, my voice raspy and tight.

"See what?" He craned in an attempt to see what I was looking at.

"The fin, the way my hair sways as if I'm miles below the surface of the sea. I can almost taste it, smell it."

"I see you, kneeling on the floor. Arie, what's going on? Maybe we should get Sanders to look at you?"

How could he not see this? How could he look in this giant mirror and not see the same thing that looked back at me: a mermaid, and not just any mermaid, but *me*. It took me a few seconds to catch my breath, and I had to blink hard, but every time I opened my eyes, I still saw the same thing. The same striking colors and shimmering light.

"Can you give me a minute alone, please?" I asked, not peeling my eyes from the mirror.

"Arie, I don't think—"

"Please, Keenan."

He hesitated for so long I thought he would protest more but he simply sighed and said, "Okay, I'll be right outside if you need me."

I waited for him to leave before approaching the mirror and sliding my hand down the glass. The mirror moved at my touch, rippling away from my hand, and when it finally settled I was no longer looking at myself, but an entirely different room. Its ceiling stretched further than the one in the basement. At the center of the room stood a golden chair covered in shells and sea urchins and starfish. Seaweed wrapped around two giant posts on either side of the seat and at the top rested seashells identical to the ones on the wall behind me. I squinted, trying to make out other things in the room when I heard a voice from the mirror.

Lights inside the mirror flickered and a man stood before me. I yelped, jumping backward into the table, nearly knocking over the candles.

"Are you all right in there?" Keenan called.

"I'm fine."

Though, was I?

The man who stood before me had my entire body shaking—my hands clammy as I moved toward the mirror once again. I don't think he could see me, because he looked outwards as if there wasn't a random girl standing only feet from him.

Everything about him screamed importance, from the way his shoulders rolled back to his puffed-up chest. Vibrant red locks covered his head and chin, hair that matched my own. Though, it wasn't his stature or even his hair that had me frozen where I stood. Emerald eyes, big and bright, but also filled with sorrow and hopelessness stared into the distance. I had no idea how I could know that from a stranger, I just *knew*. It was as though I'd known this man my entire life.

He wore dress robes, much like King Roland, only his were bright and beautiful akin to his eyes. Styled in green and blue, they sparkled against the light beaming from above. Atop his gleaming hair sat a golden crown enveloped in real emeralds and pearls. Spikes intertwined with one another like a braid as it wrapped around the front. He pressed a hand to his face, rubbing it ever so slightly until a sigh escaped. When I could see his expression again the sorrow was gone, replaced by tight lips and a furrowed brow.

"Tell me she's safe," he said, his voice deep and sharp.

"She is. Malakonius and Vikterian have it under control." The second voice came from someone I couldn't see.

Malakonius? Vikterian? He wasn't talking about *my* fathers—was he?

The man, a king, sighed a breath of relief. A tear fell down his cheek, but only one before he wiped it away and cleared his throat.

"Then seal the gates."

"What? Are you sure?"

"Do we have any other choice, Gabriel?"

"I suppose we don't. You realize if she doesn't come, if she never finds her way home, we will not be able to leave."

"We have to have faith. My daughter must find her way home. Now leave me. There's something I have to do."

Seconds passed before the king rose from his chair—his throne. He paced back and forth before looking directly at me—into the mirror, anyway.

"I don't know if you will see this, or when you will see this. But you will be grown and no longer the infant I have come to love and adore. Whenever that time comes, whenever you are standing before this message, you must know how important all of this is. How important you are. My daughter, my *Ariella*. How I long to hold you in my arms again. Come home, find your way back to me so that our world can right itself once again. I can't explain now, not when *she* lurks so close to the magic I'm using. Just follow the song in your heart and it will lead you back home. I love you. Until we meet again."

As the words trailed off, the mirror rippled until only my reflection remained. No tail, or beautiful colors, or ornate shells. Just a pirate in her pirate garb.

My heart thudded hard against my chest while my hands shook even more. I'd grown a splitting headache and couldn't process what I'd just seen, what I'd just heard.

The song in my heart? Was he talking about *that* song, the one I heard so often when near the sea? Maybe he was talking about someone else, after all he'd said Ariella, that wasn't my name.

Arie, Arie Lockwood. That's who I was. Yet, that man's words rang truer than anything in my entire life. And his eyes, his face, mirrored my own. Was he my... had I just met...? I shook my head, I couldn't breathe, couldn't think. I had to get out of here *now*.

I had to get away. I couldn't stay near that house any longer, couldn't look at it. I crawled out of the space and sprinted out of the room, passed Keenan who yelled after me, and threw open the door. The rest of the crew stood in the main room and without a word I bolted out the front door. I ran as fast as my legs allowed, my ears ringing and blocking out whatever Hook said. I cursed the world, the gods, and anything else that had forced me down this path. My legs gave out the second I reached the oak tree.

A SEA OF UNFORTUNATE SOULS

It stretched upward, well past the top of my old home. The thick and reaching branches had made for an easy escape when I was younger. Instead of climbing, I pressed my hand to the trunk. The bark was cool beneath my palm as tears continued to stream down my face, blurring my vision. But I didn't need to see to know what was engraved here.

An ache crept to my chest, the desire to curl into a ball and weep was overwhelming. I ran my hand over the engraved words, tracing the initials with my fingers and wishing more than anything that my fathers were here to guide me. I was so lost, and every time I thought I gained a semblance of control, it was taken out from underneath me.

After their deaths, Frankie and I had buried our fathers under their favorite tree. We'd spent many family dinners under its branches and even more time racing to the top. Malakai had always been the victor, though now I wondered if that would still be true. I was much faster and stronger than I was back then.

My mind flickered to the mirror and the man who resembled me. I didn't know who he was, but it was painfully obvious that my fathers had kept something from me. Since the moment I started this journey, I'd known it was going to be difficult, I never thought it would hurt this bad, too. I bowed my head, the tears dripping to the grave beneath me.

"I can't do this without you." I sank to my knees, covering my face with my hands.

"Yes, you can."

Unsheathing Slayer, I whirled around to find Hook approaching. My stomach dipped as my gaze swept over his black breeches and tunic. A strand of dark hair tumbled over his forehead as he raised his hand and hook. I blinked a few times before groaning. Why did it have to be him? Hook was the very last person I wanted to talk to right now. I'd have preferred to be left alone than let him see me like this.

"Go away, Hook." I lowered the dagger and turned back to the tree. "I don't want to talk." All I wanted to do was to sit here and forget.

"So, we won't speak," he said as his footsteps grew closer.

We stood there in silence for a few moments before Hook broke it. "How about I'll speak and you'll listen." When I didn't object, he continued. "I never knew my parents; I didn't even have adoptive parents. I grew up in… an orphanage of sorts. It was about the only family Clayton, and I ever knew. Most nights we'd pretend that our parents were adventurous pirates who couldn't take their children on their expeditions but one day they'd come back for us."

Visions of Frankie sitting on the docks of Vallarta waiting for me to return flooded my memory. How often had she sat there waiting for me to return? My chest ached at how disappointed she must have felt.

"Clayton started to actually believe it. He'd stay up staring out the window at the sea. Once that started causing restless sleep and nightmares, I told him that we weren't born from parents but the forest"—Hook let out a huff—"that we grew from the same place as the trees and the grass and the rivers. It was better believing that than the alternative. You may think all is lost, Arie, but you were lucky enough to have a loving home. Never forget that."

Hook was an orphan, never knowing the love of a parent. I had parents, people who loved and cared for me. If they hadn't taken me in, where would I be now? Would I still be the pirate and hunter I'd grown into? I watched Hook, his gaze elsewhere and realized this wasn't sympathy, at least it didn't feel that way. Hook was opening himself up to me—again. *Why?* Of all people, I figured Hook would want to keep this part of his life to himself. He'd already given me insight into it once, but this was deeper than before.

"Why are you telling me this?"

"Sometimes we need reminding that things could always be worse. I don't know what happened in there, but I can see the turmoil going on in that head of yours. Just, don't let the darkness consume you like it has me."

Hook turned and started to head back toward the house, and I nearly let him, but my mouth opened before I could stop it.

"Thank you for sharing that with me, but that doesn't really help our current situation. Not unless you can make a monster magically appear on the shores." I pointed back toward the sea.

Hook whirled around. "Maybe I can't, but I might know someone who can. Of course, I was never able to find her, and everyone I've spoken to has no idea where she resides."

"What are you talking about?"

"There's rumors of another of your kind—a sea witch. Her name is only whispered in dark corners and amongst those who search for her. She's said to make deals with people who are desperate."

Desperate. That sounded like me. "All right, so how do we find this person if you've never spoken to anyone who has?"

Hook rubbed a hand along his beard. His head perked up.

"Jameson. He might know, or one of his people might."

It was worth a shot. I'd come here in search of the Leviathan, but maybe that wasn't what Jameson meant when he said to return home? Either way I needed answers and one way or another I was going to get them.

"Tell me again," I demanded.

Jameson rolled his eyes, sinking onto a battered chair. It leaned to the side with his weight, but he stayed put. I opened my mouth to yell at him to get out of my father's chair when he groaned. "The words aren't going to change the more times I tell you, Arie. The sea witch you're looking for can be found, you just have to use your gift. Open yourself up to the magic that lives within you and ask for its aid. Sea witches have the ability to find others like them. Go to the sea and let the water guide you."

To my, and Hook's, delight, Jameson had known exactly who we were talking about. A sea witch who was known for making deals, though it came with words of warning, too. Words I was willing to ignore if it meant getting Frankie out of Khan unharmed. Whatever the cost, I'd pay it.

I nodded to Jameson and gazed out to the vast sea before me. I threw off my boots and stockings and took in a long deep breath and released it. This had to work; I'd simply ask the sea for aid as I always did and hope to the sea gods that the song would respond. It didn't always answer my pleas, but this time I wouldn't stop until it did.

The sea was catacomb cold as it lapped against my feet. Waves curled around my ankles, sending gooseflesh along my skin. Opening my awareness, I pulled on the magic that coursed through my veins. It started at my fingertips, trailing up my arms and down my torso until nothing but raw energy remained. I wasn't sure I knew what I was looking for, but sometimes just clearing my mind was enough.

Above, pillowy clouds rolled in, covering the sky in a blanket of white and I closed my eyes. The hum of the sea grew louder, making the hairs on the back of my neck stand up. The feeling surrounded me. Static built along my skin, and as I opened my eyes, it came to a crashing halt, save for something faint… a voice perhaps.

Sail the seas.

My heart leapt in my chest.

Follow the clouds.

"Arie?" Hook called from behind me.

I focused on the voice that repeated itself. *Follow the clouds, sail the seas.*

What in sea's sake did that even mean? I brought my gaze to the sky, and the pillowy clouds parted, allowing the rays of sun to cast light on the water's surface. I narrowed my eyes at the path laid out before me. Was this what the voice meant? It had to be. As I made my decision to follow the light, something inside me righted itself. As though my magic agreed that this was the way.

I pointed toward the sea's path. "There. We follow that."

IX. URSA

WE SAILED FOR A FEW DAYS, RUNNING LOW ON SUPPLIES and time. While the men had bought what they could, Claire wasn't too happy about loaning more goods without enough payment. The jewels were great, but she had a business to run and only provided us with minimal supplies. The men were growing restless, and whispers started spreading about whether we were actually going the right way.

I'd spent long hours inside my quarters trying to figure out my next move. If this sea witch proved unhelpful then I needed a backup plan and at this point that plan was going to be breaking Frankie out. I'd thought about it long and hard and considered that plan the worst one yet. Roland's castle was practically impenetrable with the number of kingsmen that roamed the grounds. I may be able to find a way to smuggle myself in but getting Frankie out would be much harder. I wasn't so sure I'd risk her life like that.

After my third day of not coming out of my quarters, Keenan had made it a point to drag me out of my hovel. Stating that, while the men valued their captain, they were becoming too restless, and things would get worse if I didn't show my face.

I opened the door to my quarters, shielding my eyes from the sun as I made my way to the main deck. The clouds still hovered, taking us further away from Vallarta, and it seemed as though they were never going to stop.

Pascal and Hook spoke in hushed tones at the helm, Hector and Nathaniel gave me sympathetic looks, and everyone else pretty much kept their heads down. What was going on, and what wasn't I being told?

Keenan led me toward the helm to join Hook and Pascal.

"So, what do we know about this witch?" I asked.

"She's known as the Keeper," Pascal started. "A woman with power, knowledge, and a maker of deals. King Roland has spoken of her a few times, but mostly that she drives a hard bargain. As far as I know, she's someone you'll want to tread carefully with. Offer her something good and I'm sure you won't have to worry."

I didn't have much to offer besides jewels and gold. Hopefully it would be enough. "She's a sea witch, too, right? Do we know the extent of her powers?"

Hook shrugged. "It varies with each story. Some say she has the same powers as any other sea witch, like storm manipulation, while others say it's much deeper and darker than that. Whatever that means."

I looked at Pascal who simply shook his head. "I know many things, little dove, but this even I do not know."

That wasn't much to go on and by the look on Pascal and Hook's face, they weren't too confident about what they were saying either. Going in blind to meet one of my kind wasn't ideal, and the further we traveled the more unsettled I became.

"When we get there," I said to Keenan, "Hook and I will go inside."

"Why him?" Nathaniel argued. "It should be one of us, someone you can trust to have your back."

"She can trust—"

"Me, Hector, and Keenan." He stepped in front of Hook, their faces inches apart. "But not you."

I'd thought Nathaniel had been getting along with Hook, or at least tolerant. It made sense. Yet, I didn't exactly appreciate being treated like a helpless child. I was more than capable of watching my own back. The other option was to take Pascal. The two of them knew of this woman and would put me at an advantage. Choosing between a captain who I occasionally battled against, and an unstable wizard wasn't that hard.

"Enough," I snapped and pushed the two men apart. Hook's chest was just as hard and chiseled as I'd imagined, the curves of his muscles hard against my palms. Someone cleared their throat and I dropped my hands.

I turned to Keenan. "Give us an hour to strike a deal and if we don't come back, I want you to take the ship and leave. If anything happens you escape and don't look back, understand?"

"Captain, I—"

"Kay, I need you to take care of this crew if something happens to me."

He nodded, and around us murmurs cut across the ship. I whirled to find several men pointing toward the eastern horizon.

Land.

The clouds above dissipated, leaving behind a clear sky as we approached what I hoped was our destination. My concerns were answered as we came closer to the island. Magic sparked in the air, trickling down my skin and settling into my bones as if it had always belonged there. Something about this place, and the magic, felt oddly familiar and I couldn't figure out why. If this wasn't the sea witch's island, I'd be very surprised.

As we made our approach, I finished giving Keenan and the rest of the crew their orders. Keenan wasn't too happy about being left behind while I took Hook along with me, but Hook had heard more about the sea witch than any of the crew. Pascal was too unpredictable and the rest of my crew were too important to me.

Hook and I, taking one of the smaller row boats, made our way to shore. The sand parted beneath my boots as we crossed the beach and headed toward the tree line.

"So, how exactly do we find her? For all we know this island could stretch for hundreds of miles." Hook brushed sand from his boots.

"I…" I stopped. My eyes pinned to the tree line where two people stood leaning against a rotted tree trunk. I squinted, but shadows kept them from seeing anything other than their outlines. I withdrew Slayer from its sheath and kept it close to my person.

Hook drew his blade as we moved further away from the water.

"Threat or no threat?"

I shrugged. "I don't know but let's make sure the only threat here is us."

Hook grunted in agreement as the men left their stump and met us on the beach.

They both wore long robes that shielded most of their faces and I wondered how in sea's sake they weren't dying of heat exhaustion. What I could see of their faces, revealed yellow eyes and jagged teeth.

"Welcome," said the man on my right. " Madam will be happy to know she has guests."

"Follow us and we will take you to her." The other man gestured toward the trees behind him.

"Yeah, no thanks."

"Arie, we don't exactly have time to look for the witch ourselves when you only gave us an hour," Hook murmured. He may have had a point but following two hooded men into unknown territory to speak with a witch seemed like a sure way to find myself in an early grave. I had no desire to die today. I glanced at Hook and then back to the men. Then again, these two didn't stand a chance.

"Take us to the sea witch, but any funny business and I'll slit both your throats before you can cry out for help." I pointed Slayer at them both.

"No need for that. But maybe a need for introductions." The one on the right stuck out his hand to which I ignored. "I'm Klaus, and this is Stephan."

Hook pointed toward me. "Arie, and I'm Hook. Can we get moving? We don't have much time."

Klaus and Stephan led us down a dirt path before it was replaced by stone slabs. Nestled beneath thick vines and covered by a canopy of trees, was the largest house I'd ever seen. Where the rock walls weren't covered in green, arched windows sat along either side of the two-story building. On either side of red double doors, were untamed bushes wild with weeds and purple flowers.

For the most part, this place appeared to be abandoned. No one patrolled the grounds from what I could tell, and with the greenery nearly engulfing the entire house, I wasn't sure we were in the right place.

"This doesn't look like some magical sea witch's house to me." Hook murmured behind me.

"Looks can be deceiving," said one of the men. I couldn't exactly tell who was who at this point and they both sounded the same.

Rather than head up the stairs and through the front entrance, the men led Hook and me around back and stopped at a side door. Stepping inside, red brick and hanging lanterns surrounded us. There were no other doors or openings that I could tell, not until we reached the end of the corridor and found a set of stairs. It spiraled downward, squeaking under our feet. The stairs finished at a dirt floor and another long hallway. This corridor revealed dozens of steel doors all equipped with a small window-like opening with three vertical bars. I tried to peer inside, but they were too dark to see into.

A cool draft wrapped itself around me as I passed pillow-like moss scaling gray stone walls and strange, curvy stalactites.

The corridor finally spilled out into a larger room that looked more like a cave than an actual room. At its center sat a large black cauldron with steam rolling from its contents. Along the furthest wall from me sat a large vanity flowing with perfumes and make-up and a mirror nearly as large as the one in the basement of my home. Large pink and purple plants sat all over the room and as the men walked forward, the plants seemed drawn to them—to us. Moving so they grazed our calves as we walked. I shivered and held my breath until we were in the next room.

Here, a woman I presumed to be Ursa sat on a large throne, her hands curled around its arms, which looked akin to an octopus's tentacles. The chair, covered in purple anemones, stretched upward to reach the top of the cave, and branched outward into more tentacles with hundreds of hanging corals. Now I thought about it, that could have been what was in the corridor as we were walking in. They appeared to be darker in color and stiffer in the corridor but here they were swaying in a nonexistent breeze. I squinted, trying to look closer and could have sworn one of them had eyes.

Ursa stood from her throne, revealing a black strapless gown that clung to thick curves. It flowed outward at the bottom; the laced-covered train followed her. White pearls hung from her neck to match the long curly hair cascading down bare shoulders. Dark eyes trailed up and down my frame before her lips curled into a smile.

"Who do we have here?" Ursa purred.

Waves of unease washed over me as she met my gaze. Static

crawled against my skin and Ursa's eyes narrowed ever so slightly. I swallowed down my fear and placed my shaking hands at my back. Being in the presence of one of my kind had my nerves in shambles. I had so many questions, so many things I wanted to know about what I was and what I could do. We'd come for help with the Leviathan, but I couldn't help the curiosity that nipped at the back of my mind.

"I'm Arie, and this is Hook," I said, pointing at him as he fidgeted next to me. His gaze traveled to each section of the room as though he were in search of something. He didn't even acknowledge that I'd said his name. I nudged him with my elbow.

"You look as though you've traveled far. Might I offer you a beverage or something to eat?" Ursa snapped her fingers and a platter of food and wine floated in front of us causing me to flinch. My stomach rumbled at the smell of stew that wafted from the ceramic bowls. As much as my insides wanted the warmth that the stew would provide, we didn't have time. We'd given Keenan an hour and I wouldn't waste a second of it.

"Uh… no thank you. I was hoping you might be able to help us." I gestured to Hook and myself.

"Well, you've come to the right place. What is it that I can do for you, Arie?" My name rolled off her tongue like honey, thick and inviting.

"We're looking for a monster that dwells in Scarlett's Lagoon, you may have heard of—"

"The Leviathan." Ursa hissed and cleared her throat before continuing. "What would two pirates want with such a deadly beast?"

I had no intention of telling this woman more than she needed to know. I was simply a monster hunter searching for a bounty, nothing more and nothing less. "I have a bounty."

Ursa clasped her hands together. "Bounty hunters, look boys, we have a couple of hunters in our presence. How exciting."

Stephan and Klaus sat on the stone floor cuddled up next to one another. One perked up and clapped. "Ooo... how exciting."

The other paled and said, "Y-You don't hunt our kind, do you?"

Huh? Our kind. Did he mean humans? "Umm... no."

Ursa shot her... minions, guards, I wasn't sure what these men were to her... a glare and they hunkered down even further to the stone floor.

Beside me, Hook stiffened.

"You'll have to excuse them; they've been hit too many times in the head." Ursa said through gritted teeth before returning her focus to me. "So, you're searching for the Leviathan, which I'm guessing isn't on its island, otherwise you wouldn't be here."

I nodded. "We've tried to locate it, but we ran out of ideas. Hook, here, said that you might be able to help locate it for us."

"Well, you shouldn't need my help dear, not with the magic that lingers within you."

I bit my tongue in an attempt to keep myself from reacting too harshly. How did this woman know about my magic? We were both sea witches, but I sensed little from her. No magic, not even the slightest hint save for the bit of static in the air. Then again, I'd never met another sea witch and what I'd learned from my books had been limited. There was no telling what kind of powers I could wield.

"What do you mean?"

"Don't tell me you don't know how to track sea monsters? A simple location spell is child's play for witches like us."

Malakai and Viktor never wanted me to learn the full extent of my magic. I had to teach myself and even that was mostly guessing. To know that this entire time I had the ability to track the monsters I hunted had my head spinning. What else didn't I know about my gift?

Pity, a witch's magic is her greatest ally. I jumped, my heart nearly leaping from my chest as a voice rattled in my mind. *You've never spoken in the mind of another before either, I take it.* Holy gods, was Ursa speaking to me through our minds? To be able to do such a thing... How did it work? What were the limits? Could I do that, too? Did I even want to? What if...

"You can't read minds, can you?" I backed away, my heart picking up its pace as I pushed all thoughts from my mind.

Ursa threw her head back and laughed. "No, of course not, we can speak from mind to mind, but only when projected. It appears there is very little you know about the powers you possess."

"I'm self-taught."

"Interesting, and where are you from?" Ursa stepped forward and the smell of lilacs filled my nostrils.

"Bellavier."

"Ah yes, I've been a few times, back in my younger days. The men there are... different from most." She winked at Hook. "You must have run into other witches there, I'd imagine."

Other witches? Ursa was the first one of my kind I'd ever met. I knew there were others, most of them living in the Enchanted Realm, but never once had I seen another while living in Bellavier. "I haven't, which is why I had to teach myself."

"And what do you know how to do?"

I stilled. I'd never really spoken about this stuff with anyone other than Keenan. Of course, the men on my crew had seen the way I channeled a storm and such, but I'd never openly discussed it. Doing so now with a complete stranger seemed wrong, yet she was like me. She was a sea witch, what harm would it be by telling her what I could do? For all I knew she could do it, too, and much better than I. "Mostly I meddle with storms and the clouds. I can create waves when there are none, and sometimes I have the ability to find my way if I'm lost at sea. Small things like that."

"Navigation recognition is not a small task, and neither is weather manipulation. It sounds like you have done a decent job of teaching yourself the basics. Are you sure you didn't have anyone to teach you? Your mother perhaps?"

I sighed, wishing more than ever that I knew who my mother was. Other than words of her demise, I didn't know anything about her. Malakai and Viktor wouldn't delve into it and asked me not to dig too deeply until I was older. I'd given them my word and had been planning to ask again soon before their deaths.

"She's dead. That's all I know."

Ursa narrowed her eyes yet again, this time her lips pursed, and she stepped away from me. "Is that so?"

Beside me, Hook grumbled, "We're here to ask you about the Leviathan, not talk about Arie's family history or lack of magical knowledge."

I'd almost forgotten he was there. He'd been so quiet, but now I wondered why he was so on edge. Did she speak to him, too?

We may be in a time crunch, but if Ursa had the ability to teach me how to track monsters then this whole thing would be done and over with much faster. I'd be able to save Frankie *and* learn more about what lay beneath the surface of my magic.

How long had we already been gone from the *Betty*? I sighed, as much as it pained me to say so, Hook was right. We didn't have time to dive into unleashing my powers, no matter how tempting it was. If we didn't show up, Keenan would either come barreling in here to save the day or leave without us. Though that didn't stop me from planning a second trip here once everything was said and done.

Digging into the pocket of my coat, I pulled out a leather coin purse. "I have payment for your services."

Ursa clicked her tongue. "While my services come with a price, jewels and gold are no good here."

"As I told you before, you'll need to strike up a deal," Hook said before crossing his arms over his chest and looking back to Ursa. "What do you want in exchange for helping us locate the Leviathan?"

"Have either of you heard of Atlantis?"

The lost city? Atlantis was submerged in mystery, a sunken city cursed by the gods. Some said it was once the wealthiest place in the seven seas. When I was little, Malakai and Viktor had told me stories about how it was actually a magical land with mythical creatures like mermaids who could wield magic like my own. I wasn't sure what a fictional place had to do with making deals, but I indulged her anyway.

"Just from stories as a child."

"Well, Atlantis is far from a fairytale, though I'd consider its king to be a nasty villain, so I suppose you could consider it as such. Either way, there's something that dwells in the city. Something that I need. Retrieve it for me, and I will show you what you seek."

Ursa wanted me to go to Atlantis. How was I supposed to swim to the bottom of the sea? I may be a sea witch, but that didn't mean I could breathe underwater, let alone withstand it long enough to retrieve whatever it was she wanted.

"How do you expect us to do that when Atlantis is said to be at the bottom of the sea?" Hook said as though he'd heard my thoughts.

"With these," Ursa snapped her fingers again, this time four pearls floated in front of me, shimmering in the light of the lanterns.

"Pearls? What good are they going to be?"

Ursa narrowed her eyes on Hook and hissed. "Are you questioning me?" The lanterns flickered as a pulse of heat rose in the air, suffocating me as it grew stronger with each passing second. Next to me, Hook coughed, bringing his hands to his throat as he fought to catch his breath.

"N-no," he croaked.

"Good." Ursa broke her focus from Hook and the threat dissipated leaving both of us gasping for breath. "I don't take kindly to those who do. Now, these pearls will allow you to gain entrance to Atlantis and will allow you to find your way back to me."

"And the underwater part?" I'd rather not drown on this little side quest.

"The pearls will be all that you need."

I still didn't understand how that worked, but I wasn't about to question her again. Rather than ask about the pearls, I settled on more pertinent information. "What do you need us to retrieve, exactly?"

"The Trident of Atlantis." Ursa said it as though I knew what that was. When I didn't respond, she rolled her eyes and grabbed something off a nearby table—a mirror. She held it up to me and I expected to see my reflection, but instead I saw what she wanted me to obtain: a large three-pronged weapon that appeared to be made of steel and covered in ornate etchings.

"This is what I need. Do we have a deal?"

I peered over to Hook who was staring daggers at Ursa, his entire body practically shaking as his hands balled into fists at his side. Ursa's ability to speak in one's mind would come in handy just then. Hook needed to cool down before he exploded. I needed Ursa to get Frankie back, and if he jeopardized that we'd be exchanging more than just words.

Ursa's offer of a bargain was tempting. How hard could it be to steal something from an abandoned city? Surely no one would be living in a city engulfed in water, could they? "Is this place heavily guarded? Where should I look for it? How long will these pearls last and why can't you just go get it? Before I strike up a deal, I need a little bit more information, please."

My heart thudded in my chest, I didn't want to offend the crazy sea witch, but I refused to go in blind. There was too much at stake, and this was my last shot. I had to do this right and obtain every ounce of information I could before barging into what was supposed to be a fictional place.

Ursa pursed her lips. "Very well. I'll make this quick. I can't enter Atlantis because I was cast out. King Rylan took more from me than you could imagine. My life, my heart, and my *child*. Giving more detail into the past is something I won't do, but know that Rylan is powerful and you must keep your guard up while in Atlantis. Last I knew, it was crawling with guards. The best way to get in and out without being seen is to stick to the shadows and keep your head down. The trident will be in a temple on the opposite end of the city." She glanced at the pearls. "Those will take you to the entrance, you won't need to breathe underwater because you won't *be* under the water. That's all the information I am willing to give you. If you want me to help you, that has to be enough. Now, do we have a deal?"

The whirlwind of information Ursa just laid out for me was a lot to take in. She just expected me to take all of this at face value without further questions. I was to use a pearl to transport myself into a potentially high security area, fetch a weapon that belonged to a king, and come back without being seen. Oh, and best of all was that the city that's submerged underwater isn't actually underwater. That one had me scratching my head. This sounded like a suicide mission worse than heading into the Leviathan's den. At least then I had more information to go on. This just seemed too risky.

I shook my head. "I don't know—"

"We'll do it," Hook blurted out. "As long as you hold up the bargain. Help us find and kill the Leviathan and we will get your stupid trident."

What in the *hells* was he doing? I shot Hook a glare, but he kept his eyes pinned to Ursa. This was supposed to be my deal to make, not his. His brother may be locked away, too, but I didn't like any of this. If we were going to jump into the unknown, I'd like to consider all possibilities beforehand.

Ursa turned toward me. "I need to hear the words, child."

This was stupid. Irrational. But Frankie's face… locked away and gods knew what was being done to her. This was my only option. Ursa was giving me the chance to succeed. A trident for a monster.

Reluctantly, I nodded. "Deal."

Ursa clasped her hands together and spun around, gliding back to her throne. "Then it shall be done. Bring me the trident and we can discuss the rest when you get back."

"How do we use the pearls?" asked Hook, and I found myself getting irritated at the way he'd completely taken over this conversation. Granted he had stakes in this too, but I thought we'd agreed I would do most of the talking. Yet here he was, practically begging to get out of here and get this over with. When we got out of here, he was going to have a chat with Slayer.

"Smash them at your feet and let the magic do the rest. Oh, and Arie, do be careful, yes?"

I nodded, as we left, wondering why she was concerned about me being careful. *She desired the trident.* I mattered nothing to Ursa, of course she'd asked me to be careful.

Stephan and Klaus escorted us back toward the beach with just enough time to keep Keenan from storming the island with Smith and the remaining men from Hook's crew.

"Everything good, cap?" Smith asked Hook.

"It will be. Let's get back to the ship and get this over with."

That was it. I grabbed Hook by the arm and yanked him around until he faced me.

"Everyone, leave. I need a word with *Captain* Hook," I hissed as he and I stared each other down. Keenan cleared his throat and gathered the crew as they retreated to the *Betty*.

I was done with this man's attitude, so the further away they got the better. Hook needed to learn that I was in charge here.

This was my ship, my crew, and my mission. It was time he learned what that meant.

X. MERMAID CITY

"WHAT THE FUCK WERE YOU THINKING BACK THERE?" I snapped, my feet digging into the sand as I paced. "You made the deal before we even had a chance to discuss things. For all you know this could be some sort of trap." I stopped pacing and stood in front of him. "This is my mission, Hook. I let you come on this trip with me because of your brother and the added manpower. You knew things about the Leviathan, so I figured, why not? You have a reason to want the monster dead as well, but that doesn't give you the right to do what you did back there."

Hook remained motionless save for the rise and fall of his chest. I wanted him to yell back, to tell me I was being ridiculous or to tell me where to shove it. He just stared at me like I was some little child waiting to be reprimanded. Well, I'd show him a reprimand.

I shoved him, his chest hard beneath my hand but I didn't relent. "Who do you think you are? We had a plan. I was to go in there and do the talking, remember? I don't need you stepping in when I have everything under control. Just be lucky none of my crew was there to watch you undermine me. So help me gods if you ever go off book like that again, I'll gut—"

"Do you ever shut up?" Hook rolled his eyes. "Ursa was trying to get information out of you, she's a witch and all witches are the same. They care about themselves and no one else. I did what I had to to get us out of there. Stop being a child and realize that I was right. Oh, and if you shove me one more time, I'll be the one who does the gutting."

I took a step back, hurt rose and fell from my chest at his words. Witches were all the same. Did he think that about me? Was I selfish? I had left Frankie behind and took off toward the unknown in search of a killer, but I'd done it because I cared. My crew was my family, and their lives were always put before my own. They all knew it. Hook was wrong.

"I'm done with this," I said and cursed under my breath at the crack in my voice. Why did his words sting so badly? "When we get the trident and free our siblings, you can take yourself and your crew and get the hells off the *Betty*. You may think I'm selfish, Hook, but at least I have a heart," I spat before taking off toward *Black Betty*.

"Shit. Arie, wait, I didn't mean…"

His words trailed off as I stormed away. I'd endure his presence on my ship and on this mission because he would aid in our success, but I was done dealing with someone who thought less of me than anyone else I knew.

Hook was a foolish, arrogant man, and I wouldn't let him stand in my way. I was going to get that trident and show him and everyone else that I wasn't some selfish little girl. I was a pirate, a hunter, and after this, everyone would know I was the one who'd killed the Leviathan.

Back on the *Betty*, Keenan pulled me aside and sat me down at our usual poker table. I gave him the rundown of my visit with Ursa. His face was neutral until I told him about Hook intervening. "Look, I know you like to do things your way and I respect that. You're the best captain I've known and most on this ship can attest to the things you've done for them, Hector and Nathaniel, especially, but that doesn't take away from the fact that Hook knows what he's doing. I'm not trying to say that you were wrong, but maybe understand that he's trying to help."

Stepping in and taking a deal that could likely get us killed, or our siblings, wasn't exactly helpful.

"I don't care about the deal he made. I mean, I do, but it's the fact that he considers himself the captain. It was my decision to make, and he took it upon himself to end the meeting before I felt comfortable enough. If anything happens to any of you, if I go to Atlantis and it's a trap… I'll lose everything and all of this would be for nothing."

Keenan understood my wariness, but he didn't understand that as a woman, I had to fight so much harder than Hook did to be respected. If he did that in the presence of a sea witch, what was stopping him from doing it in front of the crew? I'd worked way too hard to let anyone step on my toes.

"No one is taking anything away from you. Do you think maybe Hook was just trying to look out for you? Maybe he saw something you didn't."

"Why are you sticking up for him?" I snapped.

"I'm not, well... I'm not intending to. Hook may not be the captain of this ship, but he is one, nonetheless. While he may not be someone we can trust, you can't deny that he's useful. After all, wasn't he the one who'd suggested you speak with Ursa?" Keenan shrugged and patted me on the back "Just consider his reasons before stomping off and throwing him from the ship. You're an amazing person, Arie, you just need to learn to let people in sometimes. We're not all bad."

Maybe I had been harsh with Hook, though now wasn't the time to make amends and I wasn't sure I wanted to. I was unsure of how I felt about this pirate captain who'd been tossed into my life. He'd helped, been good to my men, and had proven himself quite useful. I ran a hand through my hair and let out a huff.

"I know that. Let's just move on. Will you come with me to Atlantis?" I'd originally wanted Hook to tag along, but after what happened I wasn't sure I wanted to face him again just yet.

"Don't you think I'd be better off with the crew? If I go, Hook will stay behind and be the one in charge." *Hells*, that was the last thing I wanted.

"Suck up your pride and take Hook with you. The rest of the crew is gearing up for what comes next. You'll want us all at our full strength and he may be more equipped to handle a trip to Atlantis." Keenan shook his head. "*Atlantis*. Who would have known that place was real?"

"Surely Hook has better things to do than tag along with—"

"I'd be more than happy to accompany you to Atlantis," Hook said as he entered the room, he held up his hands before I could speak. "Truce. We can discuss my transgressions later, but we both know I'm still your best defense. I've seen more things in my lifetime than any of you combined. Let me help you. I want a hand in saving my brother just as much as you want to save your sister."

Damnation. "Fine, meet me on the main deck and we'll head out."

Hook and I stood on the main deck, the crew surrounding us as we held our pearls. Everyone knew that once we were gone they were to head to Vallarta and wait for us there. I just hoped these pearls worked.

"Ready?" Hook asked. We hadn't spoken anymore about my outburst or his irrational actions, and at this moment I didn't want to. I'm sure he had his own reasons and to him they were justified, but to me he'd crossed a line.

"Yep." I tossed the pearl to the ground. It shattered and smoke ascended, wrapping around me in a cloud of gray. The smoke entered my nostrils and I sneezed. I tried to speak but nothing came out.

The air around me changed from a brisk breeze to warm and… wet? I blinked hard as the smoke dissipated and I threw a hand over my mouth. A wall of rock, kelp, and water surrounded me. I spun in a circle. Where was Hook? Had the pearl not worked for him?

I kicked, swimming toward the light of the surface. I was so far away; I wasn't sure I would make it. That worsened as the walls around me grew closer the further I swam upward. I kicked harder, faster. My chest ached, not only from lack of breath but the thought that Ursa had sent me to my death. Maybe her intention was to kill me. After all, I was a sea witch, too, maybe she thought of me as a threat and not someone who could aid her.

Shoving those thoughts aside, I pushed against the rock, hissing as a sharp edge sliced my palm. Bubbles escaped my lips as pain throbbed in my hand and blood pounded in my ears. Just when I thought I wasn't going to make it, my head popped up from the surface. I gasped for breath, sucking in as much air as my lungs would allow. The burn in my chest heightened as I grabbed the rocky edge.

Hoisting myself up and out of the water, I laid down on the cool rock and coughed. *Hells,* that could have been bad. Gathering my strength, I stood and my boots squished with each step. I tried to ignore my throbbing hand and aching chest. If I made it out of this mess alive, I was going to go on a very long vacation. I'd also have to thank Ursa for not warning me about where the pearls would drop us.

Lanterns hung along the cavern walls, illuminating the otherwise empty space. Nothing but rock and dirt surrounded me save for the small opening on the opposite side of the water. An exit.

I shivered, cursing at the bitter cold as water dripped from my clothes. I had to keep moving. And where the hells was Hook? Had he already made it out of the water? I thought about going back into the well, but I'd barely made it through the first time. I just had to trust that Hook could take care of himself.

Strolling over to the hole in the wall, I bent down and crawled through. More light filtered in from the other side as I emerged. I took a few steps before my foot slipped and bits of rock tumbled down a large pit. My chest tightened as I scurried back and drew in deep breaths. I peered down the pit, rock and darkness would be the only things to break my fall if I wasn't careful.

This was already becoming too much to handle. In just a matter of minutes I'd had two near death experiences. Turning around and going back seemed better and better every second.

A large stone bridge stood a few feet from me, connecting two sides of the pit, for which I was grateful. Another hole stretched from the ground to the ceiling across from the bridge. Tall, stone pillars sat on either side of the opening.

Was this the entrance to Atlantis?

Had Ursa been right and Atlantis wasn't submerged in water? I figured the pearls would have something to do about being able to breathe, but this didn't seem normal. None of this did.

My heart raced like the current, and I shivered again. I'd have to make this fast or I'd freeze before I even made it out.

Something grabbed my shoulder and I yelped, reaching for Slayer.

"It's me," Hook hissed.

"What the *hells*, Hook, are you trying to give me a heart attack?"

"Sorry, I didn't want to draw unnecessary attention."

I started to roll my eyes when I realized Hook's hand was still on my shoulder. My head said it was just a touch, a simple gesture that meant nothing. However, my heart threatened to burst from my chest as warmth flooded my cheeks. I looked from his hand to his eyes that stared back at me. *Gods*, he was handsome. I bit my tongue from telling him so when he took a step back.

"Arie, before we go I just want to say—"

I held up a hand. "Let's get through this and then we can sit down and talk, all right?"

Hook nodded and took the lead toward the bridge. We walked across, keeping our guard up as we continued through the tunnel of rocks. Pooling out the other head, a series of tall archways curved overhead and algae grew along the stone in thick patches. Looking up to what should have been a sky filled with twinkling stars, I found nothing but darkness. I squinted and saw the sky shimmer, like moonlight dancing along the surface. Was there something blocking the water? I'd have to ask Ursa when we returned.

Hook and I hid in the pillar's shadows when the arches came to an end. The path continued up a set of crumbling stairs. I scanned the open space for any signs of people, watching as Hook climbed two stairs at a time, skipping the ones that were disintegrating or missing.

At the top, I nearly dropped to my knees. Tattered stone buildings rose ahead, most of them missing various pieces that now lay in rubble at our feet. Stone and dirt covered the path ahead. Several columns stood along the path, and light beamed from the tops revealing more of the war zone. I looked between buildings and behind broken statues, but there wasn't a soul in sight. Whoever had dwelled here had long since moved on. Either that, or they were all in hiding.

"Ursa didn't say anything about it being abandoned. You think she knew?" Hook asked.

While this place appeared to be without inhabitants, I wasn't so sure that was true. Something pricked at the back of my neck, sending my hair on end. I whirled around finding nothing but more broken rock and emptiness.

Was someone watching us?

"I don't know but keep your guard up. I don't like this."

As we made our way through the chaos that was once Atlantis, we remained silent. The buildings thinned, leaving us to walk through a field that glowed as though it was made from jellyfish. Seagrass swayed high enough that we were able to hide within its depths. Perhaps we were at the bottom of the sea after all. It still didn't answer how this was all possible. Hook crouched beside me, still scanning the field. The feeling of being watched intensified as we climbed over a hill.

"Whoa," Hook called out ahead of me and I ran to catch up.

On the other side of the field was a large building faced with silver in its entirety. Long columns held up its roof, each one carved into some sort of statue. I narrowed my eyes; the statues weren't just of men, but men with long elegant tails. The tails curved in S shapes, while their chests lay bare save for a symbol repeated across each one. A trident.

The entire complex was surrounded by an outer wall of gold and ornate etchings. Upon the hill I could make out very little, but from what I could tell, it looked like some sort of temple.

Beyond it sat a house as large as Ursa's. I stopped in my tracks. Next to the house was a garden, bigger than any I'd seen before, flourished with plants and blossoming flowers. Towering statues stood in various sections of the garden, all of them facing my direction. A warmth enveloped me, a feeling of rightness settling into my bones and I wanted to explore every inch of this place. Though, there was something still bothering me.

Where was everyone?

Ursa had claimed that this place would be swimming with guards. We'd kept to the shadows and thankfully the field had worked as shelter, but I figured we would have seen someone by now.

"What are the odds that this trident is still here? I don't see anyone guarding that temple."

Hook grunted. "Not sure, but we'd better get moving."

Since arriving, Hook hadn't taken his hand off his blade. He may have walked with ease, but by the furrowed brow and clenched jaw, I wasn't fooled by his calm demeanor. We were both on edge and the further into Atlantis we went, the worse it got.

We kept low to the ground as we crossed the rest of the field. Only when we were close to the temple did the sound of voices stop us in our tracks. So, there were people here.

I needed to get closer to pinpoint where the voices came from. Ursa seemed adamant that stealth was my friend here and I intended to heed her warning. The seagrass thinned until it finally ended at another stone path. I slipped behind a wall and stilled as I ran a hand along it. My eyes widened. These weren't just golden in color; they were literal gold. Pure and solid and... this entire wall was worth quadruple the number of bounties I'd cashed in over the years. If they created walls out of gold, what other loot could I get my hands on?

I turned to Hook, about to speak, but his eyes were wide, and he pressed a finger to his lips.

"I don't think he's ever going to come out, Namara." A man's voice carried over the wall. We were close.

"He'd better, or I'm worried he might have a mutiny on his hands. There's too much fighting, too much animosity. We've waited too long. How can we be certain he will fix this?" Namara sniffed, her words littered with sadness.

"You just have to have faith."

"How can I possibly have faith? We're *cursed*, Samael. Nothing is going to change that, not even Kai herself will save us."

Kai? It had been a long time since any god or goddess had shown their face on earth. Even when you prayed every day for three years, sometimes twice a day, they still didn't come. Didn't care.

I'd learned that the hard way, and apparently so had these people.

My chest tightened at the thought. The one named Namara said they were cursed. Ursa hadn't mentioned that—she hadn't mentioned that Atlantis looked like a week's worth of storms had blown through leaving destruction in its wake either.

"Come on, let's get inside. Our shift is over, and I'd rather not be here when Louis shows up to take over," said Samael.

This was my chance.

The sound of footsteps vanished, and we darted around the golden wall. We stopped before a tall bronze double door. It towered over us, covered in ornate symbols. A language, maybe? With both hands I pushed it open, sweat dripping down my brow from the efforts. or was it remnants of the sea? I wasn't entirely sure.

Closing the door, I turned and found myself in an enormous room. Walls decorated with various paintings from scenery to portraits caught my eye first, followed by white-marbled floors and golden statues. The ceiling was a good thirty feet above me and covered in stained glass. A rainbow of colors danced across the floor. I found myself gaping at the statues of more merman standing in a semicircle. At the center was a small pillar, no taller than my knees. On top, sticking out, was the trident.

My heart stopped.

Hook froze next to me. "Is that?"

As if the light from the glass above was a sign from Kai herself, I slowly moved forward, one small step at a time as I admired the spectacle. It was pure and solid gold and etched with the same ornate detailing of swirls and symbols as the door.

If Keenan were here, he'd have told me to turn around and walk away, that taking something like this would be messing with unknowing forces. Even pirates wouldn't mess with the gods. Not that this trident was one of their creations, but how could I be sure when I could feel the magic roaring through it. The pulse of power intensified between me and the trident.

I couldn't afford to care. The need to get Frankie back overruled him and the gods. My hands shook at my sides, fingers buzzing with magic as I drew closer. All I had to do was curl my fingers around the golden handle and yank it from its home.

"Hurry up, there's no telling when the next guard will be here," said Hook.

I turned to Hook. "Doesn't it seem odd to you that there aren't more guards here?"

He hesitated, looking around before nodding. "You're right, something seems off. I'm going to stand watch. Be careful."

I nodded and stepped onto the small platform as Hook retreated toward the front door. I reached for the trident. The buzzing intensified as it tickled the end of my fingertips, static curled around my hands and up along my arms the closer I got. As my fingers grazed the trident, searing pain radiated from every part of my body, a jolt of electricity sending my muscles into fits of shock. My head throbbed as though it might explode, and tears welled in my eyes. I bit my tongue, tasting blood.

When the pain finally subsided, I crumbled to the ground, gasping and coughing as my heart threatened to burst from my chest. My limbs jerked against the cold floor. I couldn't move.

Was I paralyzed? No. To my relief, I wiggled my toes and fingers with only minimal pain.

"Don't. Move."

I opened my eyes to a silver spear in my face. My gaze trailed up its length to the face of the scariest man I'd ever seen, maybe even worse than the kingsman who'd hurt Frankie. He towered over me like a god, with glistening muscles and a bare chest, wearing only trousers. His dark mahogany hair was pulled back into a bun and his even darker eyes pierced me like a dagger. I tried not to squirm under his gaze.

This must be Louis.

Where had he come from? Worse yet, where was Hook? Did they already have him?

"Who are you?" Louis demanded.

"Davy Jones," I choked.

The tip of the spear touched my nose.

"I will not hesitate. Who *are* you?"

I held up my hands. "All right, okay, no need to be hasty. My name is Ar—Ariana."

"How did you get in here and where did you come from? You're not one of us, you smell..." He took in a couple deep breaths. "You smell like the enemy, yet you look like *him*."

His spear dropped away as he lowered his face closer to mine. I squirmed under his gaze, which only made me want to bring Slayer out. But I held still. Not only was he holding a sharp weapon, but he was ten times bigger than me, and I wouldn't stand a chance. Not when I'd just been electrocuted, anyway.

"It's not nice to smell your guests." I murmured.

"That implies you are here visiting. Though by the looks of it you are trespassing… and stealing our king's trident. Stand up."

I didn't have time to center myself before Louis grabbed me by the arm and I hissed. They still twitched, and even worse, my legs refused to function as he dragged me from the hall.

Ursa's intel on the trident hadn't given any indication that it was booby trapped. Another thing I would have to thank her for later. I was starting to wonder if she really was trying to kill me.

"Where are you taking me?" I asked, even though I was pretty sure I already knew the answer.

"To the king."

XI. TRIDENT OF KINGS

KING RYLAN WAS THE MAN FROM THE MIRROR.

Time had not been good to him; wrinkles now covered a sunken face and the red hair I'd admired not that long ago was now layered with gray. Dark circles lined a pair of green eyes that pierced me, as sharp as Slayer's blade.

The room spun. This man might be more than just the king of Atlantis.

Was it possible that I stood in the very presence of my real father?

I didn't know whether to curse the gods or Ursa for putting me in this situation so blindly. I found myself unable to move, unable to think. The longer I stared at his features, the more certain I became.

I blinked hard, hoping that when I opened my eyes I'd be back on the *Betty* and all of this wouldn't be real. My stomach twisted in knots as the air grew thick with tension.

King Rylan stood and paced in front of me, his walking stick tapping with each step. His robes were decorated in splashes of blue swirls, and jewels—no *shells*, hung around his neck and wrists.

He hadn't said anything since Louis had brought me here. He'd given me one look and hadn't so much as flinched. Maybe I was wrong, maybe he hadn't been talking about me in the mirror. After all, whomever his daughter was had been named Ariella. I suppose Arie was similar enough, and the striking resemblance of fiery-red hair, but then why wouldn't he be more excited that his daughter was here? What had he said? *We have to have faith. My daughter must find her way home.* So, if I was his daughter, this meeting would be much more enjoyable than this. For all I knew he could be talking about Frankie.

Solidifying that thought in my mind, I took to checking my surroundings. There were no other guards around, even Louis had retreated from the room when Rylan had entered. This was the same room I'd seen in that mirror hidden in my childhood home. Like the king, everything was weathered. Dust and grime covered the throne, seaweed and algae littered the floor. Didn't he have people who cleaned for him? Candles clustered around the room, giving the only light, but I could still make out the detailed etchings along the wall above the throne. I found myself lost in the beauty of King Rylan's throne room when he cleared his throat.

"I asked you a question."

"Sorry, what did you say?" I peered up at him; he towered over me. If I had to picture what the epitome of a god was, he was it. My stomach twisted as I fought to keep myself from squirming under the fire in his eyes.

"Why were you trying to steal the trident?"

"I don't believe we know each other well enough to begin detailing why we do the things we do. Now, if you don't mind letting me and my friend go—"

King Rylan stopped in front of me. "Who sent you?"

I kept my mouth closed, unsure of how to move forward. Ursa made it clear that King Rylan was an awful man. He'd taken things from her, her own child. How was I to believe he could be trusted with whatever I told him? I was going to have to figure a way out of this mess.

"Tell me what you did with Hook and then maybe we can talk." I was trying to stall, to figure out my next move when King Rylan slammed his walking stick down.

"You will tell me what I want to know, and your friend will not be harmed. Did *she* send you, has Ursa decided to use you against me again?"

Used me against him, what was I missing here? I clenched my jaw, keeping my mouth sealed. I had nothing to say to him. Rather than indulge him, I thought about a plan of attack. Getting the trident was still my plan, now it would just prove to be a little bit harder. It had shocked me, and my arms still stung from the jolt, so my first obstacle was figuring out how to touch it without being fried.

King Rylan continued to pace as he muttered. "Do you even realize who it is you're working for?"

I scoffed. "I'm not working for anyone. I made a bargain."

"They promised me you'd be safe. That you'd know everything when the time was right." Rylan ran a hand along his face and through his beard. "Now you're telling me you've made a deal with the devil herself. I've been waiting for her to make the first move; I just hadn't imagined it would be like this."

I tried to follow him, but he wasn't making much sense. Seeming to shake off whatever was bothering him, he strode over to the far end of the room toward a door. "I want to show you something so you can understand who it is you're bargaining with."

He escorted me out of the throne room and down a corridor that led to a large red door. His hand hovered over the knob before his head turned slightly toward me. Not quite so he could see me, but enough that I noticed the sadness that lurked in his eyes. "Beyond this door lies what's left of the Atlanteans."

The door swung open, and I froze, a lump forming in my throat as rows and rows of occupied beds came into view. Men, women, and children, lay motionless save for the rise and fall of their chests. The ones closest to me were pale, their skin wrinkled and frail as if they were wilting away. Each bed was equipped with a smaller table and a small stack of blankets.

At our approach, two women in white robes spoke in hushed tones as they checked on their patients, but neither of them regarded us. Too busy taking care of those who couldn't do so themself.

Along the far wall, a fire cracked and hissed under a cauldron. The smell wafted toward me and filled my nostrils, sending my stomach into fits. I wasn't sure why they were cooking in here, surely none of these people could eat. One of the women strode over to the cauldron and poured some of its contents in a bowl before bringing it over to one of her patients. She placed a rag inside the bowl before ringing it out and placing it over a man's forehead. Whatever it was brought some color back into his face.

Rylan made his way to the nearest bed, his hand resting on a woman's forehead. He lowered his lips and placed them on her cheek, whispering something into her ear and I looked away. An intimate moment that was meant for them and them alone.

"What happened here?" I asked, wondering now if this was where all the people had gone. How many were here? There were so many rows of beds that it would take me hours to count them all. How could two women tend to all these people?

"Ursa happened." King Rylan's voice lowered before he turned back to me. "This is what happens when Ursa doesn't get her way."

Ursa did this? My heart started to ache until I remembered what Rylan had done. He wasn't innocent in this either. "Is this what she did after you stole her child?" I asked, a bite to my tone. I felt sorry for all of these people, but I couldn't feel sorry for a kidnapper.

Rylan whirled to face me. "Is that what she told you? I took you away to protect you, to keep you alive. I sent you away with my most trusted advisors and ensured she could never find you. Yet somehow, she did. Malakonius and Vikterian are the only people I knew I could trust with my daughter."

Gods.

Gooseflesh ran down my arms and my hands shook. If my suspicions were right, that meant he was my... my knees buckled, and I grabbed the table nearest me for support. Since I could remember, I'd dreamt about this day. Malakai and Viktor were everything to me, but I always wondered what my real parents were like. I looked up at him, tears danced along his eyes as he watched me.

King Rylan *was* my birth father.

"These are good people, fierce men, strong women, and innocent children, all of them victims of Ursa's wrath. Forced to live like this because of me, because I knew what she would do to you if I didn't send you away." He ran a hand over his face. His chest rose and fell before he continued. "Being a child of a sea witch, I knew she'd be able to track you so I did what I must to ensure she couldn't. Even if it meant sealing Atlantis and possibly never seeing you again."

Hold on. Was he implying that *Ursa* was my mother? It dawned on me then... What had the siren's in Scarlett's Lagoon said? She Who Watches was looking for her daughter. Ursa and She Who Watches were the same person. Which meant she was responsible for the destruction of Hook's ship and the deaths of those men.

As if Rylan could sense my unease, he grabbed a nearby chair, and I sat. My stomach twisted in so many knots that I had no idea how to untangle them all. He'd thrown me so much information, and I had a hard time keeping up.

My entire world was crashing around me. I fought to breathe; beads of sweat traced down my face as I wiped my palms on my pants. Spots entered my vision and it felt as though a ton of bricks lay on my chest. Ursa hadn't said anything to me. She had to know who I was. Thinking back, she had been pretty interested in me and asked questions more personal than a stranger would.

"I'm sorry you had to find out this way. I don't understand why Malakonius never told you. He promised me the day I put you in his arms that when the time was right he'd make sure you knew. I guess I'll have to ask him myself."

I replayed his words and my mind and realized that he'd said that my fathers *are* the only people he trusted. Did he not know?

"I'm sorry to have to tell you this, but Malakai and Viktor are dead." Each word stung as it left my mouth. I missed them so much just then and wished they were here. Curse the gods for taking them away from me. Curse the gods again for continuously messing with my life. I should've been killing the Leviathan and saving Frankie and instead here I was, learning the truth. "Malakai never got the chance to tell me anything."

King Rylan lowered himself to the floor, his hands covering his face as he cried. The two women rushed over to console him. I looked away and allowed the tears I'd been holding back flow down my cheeks. I brushed them away and cleared my throat. "They treated me well. I have them to thank for giving me even a semblance of a happy life."

My mind was on overload, and knowing the right course of action seemed impossible, but he deserved the truth. My fathers would have wanted him to know. I let him have his moment while I tried to place the pieces of the puzzle he'd given me together. The more I mulled over what he'd said, the more confusing everything became. I needed to know more.

He lifted his head, wiping away tears. "Do you know who did it?"

I shook my head. While I wasn't sure, I did have a new suspicion. "Could it have been Ursa?"

If she'd cursed all of these people because King Rylan sent me away, what would she do to two men who hid her daughter from her for years? Though, if that were true, then why not take me upon my return? When I walked in my house there was no one there besides my family. Why would she leave if she was there for me?

"Yes," Rylan said without hesitation. "It is a possibility. I don't know how, but never underestimate her reach or her power."

"You said Ursa would do something to me if you hadn't sent me away, what did you mean by that?" I asked, hoping a change of subject eased the pain we were both feeling.

"It's complicated. The blood that courses through your veins is made of a sea witch and a mermaid. Mermaids and sea witches hold different powers, but combined they are unstoppable."

I was a *mermaid*. That meant these people really were merfolk. Malakai's stories about them were real. Did this mean all of his stories were true? My head spun and I tried to hold on to my cool, but with each word the king spoke, the more frantic I became. Everything I knew was being thrown around like a ship in a storm.

King Rylan rose from the floor, thanking the women for their help, and gestured for me to follow him back the way we'd come. "Ursa has always wanted power. Whether it was power to control those weaker than her, or actual magic. I'd been a fool, tricked by her illusions and before I saw through her ruse she was already pregnant with you. When she revealed who she really was, I knew I had to save you. There's a reason Ursa sent you here, and I'm beginning to understand why."

He didn't say anything more, which irritated me, but I tried to be patient. There was so much being thrown at me and I didn't want to miss any of it. The necessity to know all the answers was overwhelming. So much I almost forgot about Hook. I made a mental note to ask Rylan where he kept him.

We walked in silence for a bit longer and I did my best to keep my panic at a minimum. He led me outside and back through the field until we reached the temple where the trident was. Why in sea's sake would he take me back here? Rylan was silent as we entered the hall to stand before the thing I'd been sent to steal. Minutes passed by before either of us spoke.

"This trident represents more than just the king or queen of Atlantis. It's the very thing that made this incredible city. It's a symbol of honor, duty, and loyalty to the merfolk. King Atlas was granted a special gift from Kai herself; using his new power he blessed this place with the ability to flourish. Gardens that never wilted, buildings that were strong and everlasting. People who could live on land and in the depths of the sea. With Kai's guidance, Atlas gave us life. We owe it to him to continue keeping this place alive."

King Rylan turned to face me. His somber eyes glistened with tears. "Ursa is a threat that cannot be ignored. All those years ago, she'd brought you to me. You were only a few days old when she asked me if I'd take care of you both. How could I not? It wasn't until a few days later that I realized what she was doing. Every time I went to visit you, you looked paler and weaker. I called on my best doctor who'd said you were dying, as if your life force was being taken from you."

I'd almost died. I'd been in that situation before, on the brink of death as I stared down the monster I was hunting. To think I'd been dying when I was too young to do anything about it had my stomach churning.

"It took me too long to realize what Ursa was up to. It wasn't until the day she left with you *and* my trident that her plans became known. When I found out who she truly was. She was siphoning your magic to gain access to the trident, but in doing so it was killing you. If I hadn't stepped in, you'd be gone and so would Atlantis."

My own mother had tried to kill me. I didn't understand why. She was powerful, I felt it by just being near her. Why would she need my magic if we were the same? "You said mermaid blood and sea witch blood together was powerful, but I don't have mermaid magic. I don't have a tail or the ability to breathe underwater or whatever else it is they can do."

"You're right, as of right now, you don't. I had to lock that part away. It was the hardest decision I ever had to make aside from sending you away."

Desperation littered his words and I blinked away tears. Having to send away your child, to hide them away from their own mother, I couldn't even imagine the devastation he must have felt.

King Rylan cleared his throat. "Ursa needs that side of you to be able to wield the Trident. If she siphoned all your magic, she'd have the means to end us all. I think that's why she wanted you to come here. I think she planned to have us cross paths. She knew what touching the trident would do with your mermaid half closed off." He paused and ran a hand through his beard. "I believe she's planning to finally finish what she started, and that all ends with you."

Rylan placed a hand on each of my shoulders, and I fought back the bundle of emotions running through me. I'd grown what felt like a permanent lump in my throat and my head pounded. This was all too much. The same panic I'd felt when I first saw King Rylan in the mirror returned and I needed to get out. I couldn't breathe, my throat tightened, and my heart raced.

"You can end this. You can take the trident and get rid of the greatest evil that plagues the seas."

As those words left Rylan's lips, I ran.

I had no idea where I was running to, but I didn't stop until my chest ached and I was far from the temple. I reached a small alcove between a massive rock formation, the sound of water luring me further inward. To my relief, a small pool waited just a few feet ahead. Sulfur filled my nostrils and I grimaced. What kind of pool was this?

I inched closer to the water, steam rolled off the top as I slipped off my boots and stockings. With a toe, I touched it against the pool, and I yipped. A hot spring—something I was not expecting. I hissed as the water wrapped itself around my legs. The smell was awful, but the warmth settled the panic that had nearly consumed me. It gave me time to think.

Rylan had thrown an enormous amount of shit my way. From revealing my true parents, to my identity, and then to ask me to take down my own mother. It was all just... too much. I didn't want any of this. Not the history lesson, or the insight into who I really was.

As a child you were expected to trust that your parents had your best interest at heart, that they knew what they're doing and as long as you listened to them, everything would be okay. What happened when your entire life was a lie? When the ones you were supposed to feel the safest with spend your entire life lying to you? Malakai and Viktor had loved me, this I know, but not once did they tell me I was different. They'd shielded me from a life I deserved to know about. Sure, they'd hinted at a few things, like the fact they weren't my real parents but I was so loved and one day everything would make sense. Or that I would grow up to be more than they could ever imagine. None of it made sense then, not until now.

A scream escaped me as I drove my fist into the ground. Everything was a complete and utter mess. Frankie was waiting for me, and I still had no idea how to save her. My own mother wanted to take my magic, which would kill me. She also wanted the trident, but if I gave it to her, she'd continue to hurt innocent people. Rylan wanted me to kill her for what she'd done and if I didn't kill her, she'd siphon my magic without second thought. I had to make a decision and the clock was telling me my time was up.

Covering my face with my hands, I let out a long-exasperated sigh.

"Sounds like you could use a drink."

I stumbled out of the spring and found Hook a few feet away with a bottle in his hand. A part of me wanted to yell at him to go away, that his company wasn't wanted or needed, but the other part of me thought I could use the help deciphering what to do next. Hook was a pirate, a man who'd fought and killed and his past was just as messed up as mine. Two minds were better than one and at least his opinion wouldn't be biased.

"Where have you been and how the hells did you find me?"

"The king had me locked in a room with Louis. He came to me, asked me where you might run off to. Figured you'd find your way to water, and he told me where to go." I was surprised Rylan had allowed Hook to leave without a guard or anything. I peered around but it was only us. Even more surprising was that Hook knew where I'd be. The bottle of whatever he had sloshed as he came closer, and I held out my hand.

"Give it," I said as Hook passed the bottle. I held it to my lips, letting the liquid slide down my throat. Peach wine. Damn, this was good.

"Want to talk about it?"

Handing the bottle back to Hook, I retreated to the spring and shrugged. "I wouldn't even know where to begin."

Hook threw off his boots and sat next to me, hissing as he placed his feet next to mine. "So, start from the beginning."

I skimmed over most of the non-important things like how my fathers lied to me. Hook kept his gaze forward, for which I was thankful, I didn't want his sympathy. When I was done, I was breathless and angry again. My hands shook and I shoved them between my knees.

"I knew something was wrong with her." Hook said and took

another drink. "The way she asked you those questions and the vibe I got. I've been to a lot of places, seen a lot of things, but never had I felt so on edge as I did in her presence."

I turned to him. "If that's the case, then why the hells did you want to accept her deal?"

"While I knew something was off, I also believed she really was our only shot. My plan was to kill her anyway, so what did it matter that we went and got the trident?" He'd said the part about killing her so nonchalantly that I couldn't help the laugh that flew from my mouth.

"When were you going to let me in on your little plan?"

Hook's eyes met mine and I swallowed, my throat suddenly tight. His chest rose and fell in a long, slow breath. Then he blinked and sighed. "I was trying until…"

Until I'd let him have it. "I'm sorry, I shouldn't have been so rash. I had to fight my way to captaincy. I spent most of my time at sea trying to win over an entire group of men who didn't want to give me the time of day." Keenan had been my savior through all of it, and had taken me under his wing. He'd shown me how to lead, but that bit of information didn't seem important just then. "When they finally learned to respect me and see me as more than just some little girl seeking revenge, I made a vow to never let anyone step over me. I had to show I was strong and bold, and no one was going to take that away from me. So, when you took over…" I shrugged.

Hook nudged me with his shoulder. "I get it. You like to be in control and when someone threatens that it feels like that control slips away. Just like now. Your father and your mother are at war with one another and you're at the center of it all. Yet, no matter what you do or what plan you make, you can't control the situation the way you need to."

I opened my mouth to object, but I had nothing to object to. "So, what do I do?"

"I think only you can decide that, but if it helps, I do have something to say. From what I can tell, I think you're pretty damn lucky."

Lucky? The only thing that was lucky was that after all these years I'd managed to stay alive. Now I wasn't so sure how much longer that was going to be the case. All my luck was wearing out and fast.

"You were able to grow up with a family who cared about you, who read you bedtime stories and spent every day ensuring you were happy. You had two fathers, and from what I've heard, they were good men. Not everyone gets those luxuries."

I wanted to pry, but it wasn't my place. If Hook wanted to tell me more, he would. Until then I sat there waiting for him to continue.

"I grew up with brothers and sisters. None of them were blood relatives, we were all orphans and somehow we made that work for us. It took me a long time to come around to them. Clay and I were cast aside by our parents. I found out both had died a few years later. The Lost Boys took us in, and we never looked back. Once they started finally growing on me, I found that I didn't need parents. I had everything I could ever want. Until one day it was taken from me. Clay and I left in search of a brother who had gone missing, but we were never able to find him."

I recalled our conversation from before. The one where he'd told me about wanting to get back home.

"Is that why you want to get back, to be with your family?"

Hook rubbed his face. I reached for his arm but stopped short. Would he welcome my touch? Not wanting to chance it, I slid my hand back between my knees.

"I've been gone so long. I don't even know if they'd recognize me anymore. I'm not sure I recognize myself at this point. There's so much blood and death on this hand and hook," he said, turning his palm face up, "I'm not sure they'd want me back."

"You never know unless you try."

Hook huffed. "I've tried for a long time to find my way back, and the only person who knew how to get there was the brother I searched for. I never found him and it's likely he didn't live through what happened to him. So, I took to becoming a pirate and the rest you know."

Captain Hook had just given me a full look into his past, but why? Hook wasn't just opening up to anyone, he was opening up to someone he wasn't fond of. Though, maybe this trip had brought us to be more acquaintances than anything else.

"Why are you telling me this?"

"Because I want you to see how important it is that you see how much people care about you. I've never seen a more loyal and loving crew as yours. The way they look at you, the way they throw themselves into danger for you... I envy that."

My jaw dropped slightly. Hook *envied* me. "Hook, I—"

"Just listen. I also am a pretty good judge of character. I only had to speak to Rylan for a few minutes to know that he cares about you.

When I looked at Ursa, I saw none of that. If anything, I saw hatred. With the king it's more than that. I see a father who wants his daughter to succeed. I think you should finish hearing him out." Hook got out of the water, slipping his boots back on before holding out his hand to me. I stared at it for a minute, and he grumbled, "I'm not going to bite, Arie. For once in your life have a little faith in something that isn't your blade."

I rolled my eyes and took his hand. "Where are you taking me?"

"Back to the king. If there's one thing I've learned about you, it's that you'll never let innocent people die. Your men made that very clear. You already knew what you were going to do, you just needed someone to nudge you in the right direction."

A smile crept to my face, and I did my best to shield it from Hook. I'd never seen this side to him before and while it was weird, a part of me liked seeing him like this. Though, poking the bear was far more fun.

"When did you become Mr. Know-It-All?" I smirked.

"The day I was born." Hook winked at me as we made our way back to the temple.

I swallowed down the bit of panic that rose again and let everything Hook said sink in. It was no secret that I liked to be in control and hearing it from Hook may have struck a tiny nerve. But ever since I lost my fathers everything had been so jumbled and without control, I'd have lost myself to the darkness a long time ago if I hadn't done something about it. I just had to make sure I did the right thing. Right now, that was going back and facing Rylan.

Finding a way to take down Ursa was crucial. I wasn't sure I could kill my own mother, even if she had cursed so many people, they were all alive. Though, how was I to know for sure? Pushing that aside for now, I decided to finish listening to Rylan before I made any real plans.

We stopped at the temple doors, and I tugged on Hook's arm. "Hold on a second, before we go in there's something I'd like to say to you."

Hook stayed silent, letting me have his full attention—something else about him that I liked. Since when did I like *anything* about Hook? I had to admit that having him around these past few weeks was well worth the headache he'd caused me. He'd proven useful and his crew seemed to fit in well with the others. I knew eventually, once this was all over, we'd go our separate ways, but he still needed to know that I appreciated the help.

"You've been a real asset on the *Betty*, and as much as I hated the fact that you were on *my* ship, I'm glad you were. I don't know what's going to happen next, but whatever it is, our crews will do it together."

I half expected him to roll his eyes or give a snappy retort but instead he simply nodded and led the way into the temple.

King Rylan stood next to the trident. His shoulders stiffened, but he remained where he was. I didn't know where to start or how to apologize for leaving the way that I did. He'd only been trying to tell me what I should have been told a long time ago. It was an honor to be a part of a family with such wonderful history, and one day I hoped I would have the opportunity to learn more about it. Until then, I settled on getting all the information I could regarding Ursa.

"Arie, I'm so sorry, I didn't—"

"It's okay," I said to Rylan, leaving Hook behind as I approached him. "This is all a lot to process, and I don't exactly process well."

"I understand, and before you make up your mind on what you're going to do, there's more I need to tell you. Something that's the most important piece of the puzzle."

I narrowed my eyes, what more could he possibly tell me? Did I have a long-lost sibling that wanted to kill me too?

"The monster you know as the Leviathan? Here in Atlantis, we simply call her Ursa."

XII. UNBOUND

FAINTING SUCKS.

Lucky for me, Rylan had kept me from smacking my head on the stone floor. When I came to, I was lying on a cot with both nurses from earlier on either side of me.

"Arie, are you all right?" Hook asked, his hand gripped my arm, firm and strong sending my pulse surging. Swallowing, I nodded.

"Just a simple faint." One of the nurses spoke in hushed tones. "You overloaded her with too much, Rylan."

"I'm sorry, I don't know what came over me," I murmured.

I stilled then as the memories of what had caused the fainting spell sprang to life in my mind. Ursa was the Leviathan. The Leviathan was Ursa. *Holy Gods*. Of course, the Leviathan fed off the souls of its victims; Ursa fed off the life force of hers. Souls and life force were one in the same. She used those souls to harness her powers. All those lives lost were by her hands. My mother wasn't just a sea witch who wanted to kill me, she was a bloodthirsty monster. How was that possible?

"How is it that Ursa became the Leviathan?" I asked, trying to sit up and regretted it when I had to swallow down bile. Blood pounded in my ears and my head spun.

"Eat this, it'll help." One of the nurses handed me a piece of chocolate and I shoved it in my mouth, thankful to have something in my stomach. When was the last time I'd eaten?

"The souls she takes, it comes with a price, one paid in the worst of ways. With each soul she consumes the more tainted her vessel becomes. Before long, the souls will fade to darkness and the Leviathan will be all that's left of her. To combat that, she needs a way to harness the souls without it also consuming." Rylan snapped his fingers and the trident appeared in his hands. I blinked, once then twice to ensure I wasn't seeing things. "The trident will allow her to have complete control over the beast within, but she can't touch it until she has your powers. However, there may be a way to stop it all if I open up your other half."

I stepped away from him. "No. If you open that side of me, you're just playing into what she wants. If I stay out of her reach, she'll never be able to get it. I can find a different way to save Frankie and we'll just sail as far from here as we can."

"Frankie?" King Rylan asked and I realized I hadn't told him about her. So, I explained what had caused this entire mess and that seemed to spark something in Rylan's eyes. "She will never stop coming for you unless you stop this. Frankie, your crew, Hook, everyone you know and care for will be forced to run unless you end this."

Damnation. He was right, Ursa didn't seem like the type to stop simply because we ran. If Ursa turned into the Leviathan completely, I could always return and slay the beast, but during that time what kind of destruction could she cause? How many more lives would be taken because I was too scared to do something about it now? And *hells*, I was scared. Sweat covered me, and my heart thumped so hard it nearly leapt from my chest. If I went after Ursa, I was going to have to open myself up to something new and I had no idea what to expect. But it had to be done. "All right, let's do it."

"You're ready to open yourself up to the mermagic and take on your mother?" Rylan asked.

"No, but it's the right thing to do." There was no point in lying when both men knew how I felt. I made a promise to Frankie to fix all of this, and I intended to do just that, even if it meant I wouldn't be the same after.

"This isn't going to feel pleasant. Closing it off when you were an infant was painless because it didn't have time to attach itself to you. Now, it has had time to weave its way through every muscle and bone in your body. Your soul is wrapped in its web as the magic builds power. When we unleash it, there's no telling what will happen so it's best we do this outside."

Well, wasn't that disconcerting? I was a ticking time bomb of magic and with the right poke I'd burst like a bubble. King Rylan escorted me and a very quiet Hook outside. Once we were far enough away, standing in the middle of an open field, Rylan stopped and turned around. The trident laid in his outstretched hands.

"Place your hands over the trident and above mine, but don't touch it yet."

I did as he asked, letting my hands hover over the trident. Its golden hue seemed brighter out here under the darkened sea. Suddenly my fingers vibrated, a tingling sensation slid down each one and rested in the middle of my palm. I looked up at Rylan, but his eyes were closed.

"Close your eyes, Arie, and clear your mind. Think of nothing besides the breath in your lungs and the emptiness that surrounds us. Hook, you may want to take a few paces backward."

Light footsteps sounded behind me and I couldn't resist the smile that crept to my lips.

Inhaling, I closed my eyes and exhaled slowly, I pushed all thoughts from my mind and focused on one breath at a time. There was no breeze or rustling of trees, nothing but silence as I concentrated. Viktor had taught me how to do this as a young teen. We'd sit out on the grass near the sea, and he'd ask me to listen to nothing but the waves, to shove everything from my mind and think only of the rising tide. This time though, I only had the silence.

"Good, yes, keep that up. Now I want you to search for the magic that's locked away. Feel yourself draw on that essence. You may not know what you're experiencing or even looking for, but trust your instincts and let them guide you. It's going to be new and very potent when you do find it. Be careful not to pull all the strands of your bindings at once."

How was I supposed to search for something I didn't even know was there? *Focus.* Okay, I could do this, after all, it couldn't be that different than pulling on my witch magic. I just had to decipher which one was which.

I pulled on the energy of my gift, feeling each beat of my heart and pulse of blood as I called it out. A familiar heat slid its way across my body to stall at my fingertips. If we were on the *Betty*, clouds would be rolling in, but that wasn't the magic I needed right now. Pushing that aside, I searched deeper and wider. A sea of black surrounded me. I looked for anything that appeared out of the ordinary and was only answered by the sea witch.

My witch magic usually felt like static pulsing against my skin, as if the air around me was full of electricity. As I dived deeper into my subconscious, that withered away leaving behind something new.

I shivered as cool liquid curved along my shoulders and it cascaded down my frame. The brisk chill that accompanied it sent gooseflesh down my arms. A bright blue-green light engulfed my vision, even with my eyes closed, and all I saw was blue and green flecks. The light grew brighter until the liquid covered me from head to toe. I peered down at my arms, but there was nothing there.

When I returned my gaze to the abyss, there before me was a bright blue orb, pulsing and sputtering against strands of rope that tied it together. I pulled at the strands of the bindings that surrounded the flecks. As each one broke free, the orb grew brighter and bigger until it was so bright I had to shield my face. The final piece broke free, and the orb crashed into me and I cried out. Pain forced its way along my skin. My body rose in the air as a tornado of color spun around me. The magic pricked my skin like tiny bee stings. Something connected with my palm, and I wrapped my fingers around it. Instantly the magic shattered and I fell to the ground, one knee on the grass while the other bent. I pushed myself up with whatever I held.

"*Hells*, Arie, you look… you're…" Hook's eyes were wide and his jaw wider.

"She's magnificent," King Rylan finished. "It appears the trident has accepted you, good."

I narrowed my eyes at him only to realize the trident was no longer in his hands. I dropped my gaze and, in my grasp, there it was, but that wasn't all. My entire body glowed in shades of blue and green. I shot a look at Rylan who sucked in a deep breath and let it out. I followed suit, centering myself as the glow faded.

"That was… intense." I said, the euphoria of the mermaid magic still blazed within me. It was potent, as though it still needed to unleash itself in the worst way. Maybe that would come in handy. For now, I focused on Rylan.

"It's going to take you a while to fully grasp this new part of you, but give it time. First things first, you must remember that Ursa cannot get her hands on this trident, because if she does there'll be no stopping her. If you have no other choice, then you must run. She will use it against you and everyone in her path. This is your best defense against her so use it wisely and be careful. The rest is up to you."

I hadn't expected to cry, yet tears slid down my cheeks. Rylan wiped one of them away and smiled at me. "You are more brave and worthy than I could have ever imagined. Good luck, daughter."

I nodded and turned to Hook. "Ready?"

He smiled until his dimple appeared and my breath hitched in my throat. "Let's go kill us a murderous-witch-beast."

We stood at a wall. On the other side water shimmered as though calling me. I hadn't had time to ask Rylan about the song I'd been hearing all my life and decided that it would be something to ask him when this was all over. I wasn't dying today or any time soon. I would come out of this on top and free my sister. All of this was going to work out. It had to. I turned back to Hook and Rylan.

"What about Hook?"

Rylan had said that it would be a good idea for me to travel to Vallarta with my new gift. To give myself a chance to feel what it was like to be a mermaid before having to use it against Ursa. Which made sense, even if my nerves were running rampant right along with my beating heart.

"Hook will be in Vallarta well before you will. He'll give word to your crew about what's to come, so they will be ready for you when you arrive. It won't take you long with the trident." I looked at the necklace that hung from my neck: a silver chain with a small nautilus shell. A bit of illusion magic Rylan had shown me how to work. It would conceal the trident and keep unnecessary attention away.

"Here goes nothing then." I faced the wall of water. Stepping closer, I reached out to the source of my power. With the trident's strength, nothing could stop me. I'd gather the troops in Vallarta and head off to slay the monster.

To kill my mother.

My hand touched the water first, the water split over my fingers like a motionless waterfall. I sucked in a deep breath and walked the rest of the way in, the sea taking me as Atlantis faded away.

Sparks of blue light danced at my feet, twirling and shimmering against my skin. I was instantly hit with a sense of rightness, and warmth, and something I couldn't quite figure out. The magic that bound me was broken and with that my mermaid half sprang to life. A horrible, burning sensation throbbed in my neck. I cried out and threw my hand over the skin and came back with clean fingers—no blood. What the *hells* was happening? Grazing the spot once more, my fingers slid against three long, pulsing slits. The pain subsided and I realized the slits reminded me of gills. I froze. Did I have fucking *gills*? I parted my lips, but rather than sucking in water, I was breathing.

I clasped a hand over my mouth as my gaze fell to where my legs should have been. Instead, brilliant blue and purple scales erupted from my skin, flowing up and over until all that was left was a long tail that curved at the end, the tips like ribbon trailing behind me. I ran my hand along the scales. They were not like the scales of a fish, but soft and warm.

Bracing myself, I kicked as hard as I could, which was clearly a mistake because I tumbled forward, my arms flailing as I tried to grab hold of something and found… fins?

I looked to my right and froze. A great white shark swam next to me, regarding me as I straightened. Slowly taking my hand from its fin, I tried to move back, but I didn't know how. Didn't this damn mermaid thing come with instructions? What had Rylan said? *Use your instincts.*

The shark swayed back and forth, continuing to watch me, rather than open its giant mouth and swallow me whole. I knew that wasn't possible but at that moment, logic was completely out the window. Monsters were easy to take down, but usually I was aboard my ship. This time all I had was the trident.

The trident. *Of course.*

I held the necklace in my hand and before I could make it do anything, the shark darted toward me. I shrieked, bubbles forming from my mouth, but rather than teeth sinking into me, the shark only pushed. Its head centered at my back, it pushed me forward until we were moving at such an alarming speed I was afraid of tumbling.

The shark was helping me. But why?

Sharks are a part of the same waters that a trident wielder commands. A woman's voice startled me. The whisper in my mind was so much stronger than it had ever been before.

We are finally connected, it has been a long time coming, but it feels good to finally be able to speak to you like this.

Who are you? I asked.

Think of me as a guide, someone who wants to see you succeed. Take care now, Ariella, descendant of Atlas, and always know that I am with you.

I wanted to ask more questions, but then the shark rose higher until the seabed vanished leaving nothing but a vast space of emptiness. There wasn't anything in my entire life that had felt this right. I spread my arms, taking in the glorious ride and let the shark guide me.

I tried to wrap my head around the voice and wished I'd have asked Rylan about it sooner. Before it was just a hum, a soft song on the wind that called to me when I was near the sea. But now it—*she*—spoke actual words. I would talk to Rylan about it the second the opportunity presented itself.

After what I assumed were a few hours, the shark stopped and swam around me. A dull throb pulsed in my limbs, and my eyes grew heavy. I needed sleep, and probably a good meal if we were going to take down Ursa. The shark's fins and tail moved with the current, its body slithered like a snake. What was it doing? It nudged me with its nose, sending me tumbling again until I pushed my tail, mimicking its movements. Was it showing me how to swim?

I held out my arms and pumped, but soon realized I didn't even need to do that. My tail took control, guiding us as we broke through the surface. To my delight, I was near an island where a cluster of ships bobbed along the docks. Vallarta. I smiled as the cool air wrapped around me, sending gooseflesh down my arms. I turned and thanked the nice shark before doing my best to move forward. It took me a few tries, most of them causing me to do forward somersaults, but by the time I reached the shore I'd stopped tumbling. As my tail scraped the bottom, it split in two. Pale skin replaced the scales until all I could see were human legs. I sighed a breath of relief. It was thrilling to be a mermaid, but I much preferred my legs.

As my feet touched dry sand, I noticed that not only were my boots back on, but all my clothes were on too. The only evidence that

I had been in the water was my dripping hair, which I wrung out. I was going to have to get to my ship and brush it before it turned into one giant ball of fuzz.

I glanced at the ships and was happy to see the *Betty* docked. Now it was time to find my crew and take on the mighty beast of the sea.

The Ugly Duckling had a closed sign stuck to the door, though I heard the voices of my men and pushed inside. At my entrance, Kay and Hook approached, both giving me worried glances. Before I could greet them, Keenan flung his arms around me as he spoke. "Thank the seas you're okay."

"You okay?" asked Hook at the same time.

I laughed, and hugged Keenan before stepping back. "Honestly, I don't exactly know how to answer that question. Give me a drink and a good night's rest and then ask me that." I smiled and tried to ignore the flutter in my stomach. Maybe I was hungry. *Hungry for a male's touch.* I cursed under my breath and turned to Keenan.

"How's the crew?"

He shrugged. "We're trying to keep the peace between both crews, but it's getting worse the longer we stay together. Some of Hook's men took off, but that was to be expected."

I looked at Hook. "You okay with this?"

"Any man who doesn't stay is a coward and not anyone I'd want on my crew anyway. To hells with them." Hook took a sip from his mug.

"Did Hook fill you in about everything?" I said to Keenan as my eyes landed on Hook who had returned to the bar.

"Ursa is the Leviathan."

I nodded. "We're going to have to end this once and for all. We can't let her continue to terrorize the seas. I don't exactly know what the plan is, but we can figure it out on the way."

"We have a little bit of time, you've been through a lot. Let's drink and eat and tomorrow we will set sail."

Eating and drinking sounded lovely, but I wasn't so sure that was a good idea. I shook my head when Hook appeared with two drinks in his hand.

"Hank wanted me to give this to you." He handed me a mug, and I hid my smile behind it as I took a drink. Thoughts of the pools in Atlantis flooded my mind. His gentle touch, the concern for me and the way he opened up. A part of me wished he'd never told me any of it. This man had been my rival for years, we'd fought, stolen jewels and doubloons from one another, and had hated being in the presence of the other. Yet, now I wondered what he looked like without a shirt on, or what his lips would feel like if pressed to mine.

For sea's sake, Arie. Keep it in your pants.

I cleared my throat. "I don't know, I'm pretty tired."

"Did Captain Arie Lockwood just say she was too tired to drink?" Hook's brow rose causing that flutter to continue and I cursed. Snatching the drink from his hand, I swallowed down as much of the alcohol as my body allowed. Maybe the ale would be enough to drown the thoughts of Hook from my mind.

"All right, fine," I huffed. "Just a few drinks and some food and then as soon as dawn comes over the horizon, we set sail."

Hank kept the pub closed while the crews danced and sang and ate. My men and Hook's, the ones who cared enough to stay, were becoming closer than I imagined. I watched as they chatted and laughed with one another. Some played poker in the far corner, while others were doing something odd with a knife and their hands. This was exactly what being a captain was about for me. To have a crew who were family, who stuck by you and had your back. While at one point I would never have trusted Hook or his men, now it was as though they belonged with us.

As if the thought had called Hook to me, he sat across the table and slid another mug my way.

"If I didn't know any better, *Captain Hook*, I'd say you were trying to get me drunk."

Hook smiled, his dimple deepening. He placed his arms on the table and leaned closer. His voice was husky as he spoke. "I just saw a lady without a drink in her hand and wanted to be polite."

I threw my head back and laughed. "Right."

"Arie?" I whirled around to find Jameson behind me. "A word?"

I gestured for him to take an empty chair and he sat.

"I've updated the Brotherhood of what's transpired so far. They want me to inform you to tread carefully. While they know some of what Ursa is up to, they fear that a war is brewing and you're at its core."

"A war?" asked Hook.

"The Elders aren't always keen on sharing the details, but yes, one that is much bigger than what you are dealing with. All I can tell you is that the Elders are keeping a close eye on what happens here and that Ursa's death is vital."

Fucking cryptic assassins.

Whatever the Brotherhood was up to wasn't my concern just then. Jameson was right, stopping Ursa and her war against Atlantis was what mattered most right now. I shoved what Jameson said to the back of my mind and let myself enjoy the rest of the night. After all, it might just be my last.

Day turned to night as my crew continued their fun, Hook and I were in the middle of a game of poker with Hector and Nathaniel, and Keenan was off with Smith talking about gods knew what. I checked on both crews, all of them in chipper spirits even though they knew what tomorrow would bring. Everything was finally falling into place and when the sun rose tomorrow, we'd be on our way to kill the biggest monster I'd ever faced. Though there was one face in the crowd of people I didn't see, and come to think of it, I hadn't spotted him all evening.

"Hector, where's Pascal?"

The door to the Ugly Duckling flew open, slamming hard on the wall behind it. Several men bustled in, all sorting red and black coats with the kingsman medallion sewn on the front. I swore as we all drew our weapons. More than a dozen men piled into the pub and behind them, stood Pascal. He kept his head up as he weaved his way through the crowd until he reached our table.

"Well, hello there, little dove. I was hoping you'd be in here." Pascal slid into an empty chair as two kingsmen flanked him. Both looking on as if they couldn't be bothered by my presence.

"Pascal, what's going on?" This was no ordinary visit. Kingsmen didn't just travel to Vallarta for no particular reason, and the longer they all eyed my crew, the more worried I became. The king must have sent them, but why? I narrowed my eyes on Pascal.

"King Roland would like a word."

"Roland's in Vallarta?" A vein popped out in Hook's neck as his lips tightened.

"Of course not. He sent word, and his men, to bring you back. It's my duty to do as Roland asks, or did you forget why I was on your ship?"

I stilled. Anger rose within me, my hands curling around Slayer as the wizard picked at his nails. Just when I thought Pascal and I had an understanding, when I even started to consider him something more than just the scary wizard of Khan... He'd risked his life, given us advice, and ensured we were on the right path. Now he was bringing me back to Khan for what?

"Pascal, we've figured out where the Leviathan is. We're setting sail in the morning to take it down and Roland will have what he wants. We still have a few days left, so why does the king want to see us now?"

Pascal's eyes glistened for a brief moment before emptiness replaced it. He stood and cleared his throat. "I guess you will have to wait and see what the king wants upon our arrival."

Without warning, Nathaniel shot forward. He raised his sword above his head as he charged at Pascal. My heart sank to my stomach as Pascal ducked away and grabbed Nathaniel by the arm. He pinned him against the table and held him down.

"That wasn't smart." Pascal snatched Nathaniel's dagger from its sheath and held it against his throat. "Did you forget who I was?"

Nathaniel squirmed. "Piss. Off."

Hells, what was he doing? I gave Hook a worried glance who shook his head. He knew what I wanted to do and even though it would be stupid to attack now, Nathaniel wasn't a match against the wizard. I had to protect my men.

"Let him go."

Pascal stiffened before turning to me. He took the butt end of the dagger and smashed it over Nathaniel's head. He dropped to the floor and I blew out the breath I held.

"Drop your weapons, " said one of the kingsmen.

Around us, the guards held their pistols at both crews. All eyes fell on me, waiting for me to make the first move. I hated that it had to come to this. We could fight, but I wouldn't risk another life like that. I slammed Slayer down on the table and the rest of my men followed suit. The weight of their gazes were heavy on my chest as we were escorted from The Ugly Duckling. Hank called after me, saying he'd look after *Black Betty* and that everything was going to be okay. I wasn't so sure. Without the leviathan's head or the missing cargo, King Roland would do what he promised. We were headed to our deaths.

I cursed under my breath; we should have left earlier rather than staying here. Now we were going to have to come up with a plan that involved escaping an impenetrable castle with kingsmen lurking at every turn.

I've failed.

The king would kill Frankie, and with that thought, I let defeat settle in as we boarded one of King Roland's ships. This was going to be a long trip back to Khan, and I had no idea what would come, but I couldn't give up. I felt defeated now, but I refused to believe this had all been for nothing.

I clutched the trident in my hand, the nautilus shell pulsing under my grasp, and settled in for whatever might come next.

I sat across from Pascal; his head cocked to one side as he strummed the strings of a guitar. He hadn't said anything when a kingsman brought me in. I figured he would have thrown me down in the cell with the rest of the crew, but he'd summoned me here. I was particularly surprised that he hadn't bound me to the chair or asked one of the kingsmen to stay. Then again, the Wizard of Khan may not need anything to keep me from slitting his throat. I'd seen a small glimpse of what he could do against a group of sirens, but we'd never pitted our powers against each other. He took Slayer, but *I* was much deadlier than my blade and we both knew it.

My eyes fell on the long scar across his face, the pearly eye, and his crooked nose. He looked as though he'd fought his way through hell and back and lived to tell the tale. I had started to feel sorry for him, for being a puppet to the king, but now all I wanted was to strangle him until there was no smirk left on his face. Why would he do this? What could he possibly gain from being the king's dagger? Maybe he didn't have a choice.

"It's not polite to stare."

"I'm just thinking of all the ways I'm going to kill you when this is over." The hurt I'd felt when he showed up to bring me in was new to me. Not that I'd never hurt before, but that Pascal could affect me in such a way. I knew he was this dark predator who'd done even darker things for the king, but over the last few weeks I'd started to see something else inside him. A light that wanted so desperately to break free.

He'd said he was on the *Betty* because of the king's orders, and I believed that rang true for quite some time. Yet, by the end there was more to it than that. I could see it every time he shifted his gaze from his guitar to me. He may not want to admit it, but my crew had gotten to him, and I was determined to pull on that part of him to get us free. This wasn't over, not by a long shot.

Pascal *tsked*. "Always so much fight in you. Good, you're going to need it."

"What do you get out of all of this?"

Pascal's lips widened to a toothy grin. "The pleasure of being in your company, of course."

"I mean what do you get out of turning us in? Can't you just give us a few more days? I have the location of the monster and the means to kill it. Pascal we've come so far, to just turn back now when we are so close is foolish."

Pascal gave out a menacing laugh. "I get nothing but the pleasure of knowing I pleased my king and my kingdom. I live to serve and owe my allegiance, my life, to the king and him alone. Without him I wouldn't be the wizard I am today. You should know how that loyalty feels. After all, I don't think I've ever seen so many people faithful to a hunter."

"My men are loyal to me because I treat them with respect. We have saved each other's lives countless times. None of us torture and kidnap and kill unnecessarily."

Pascal lowered his guitar and leaned forward. "King Roland does what he does to ensure the people of Khan are safe. He saved me from torture and pain and…"

He trailed off, mumbling under his breath.

Pascal's reputation for insanity and darkness he plagued the world with was known across the seven seas, but what they didn't know was that down deep there was much more to him than that. He'd saved my life, saved my men against the siren attack and had gone farther than his duties required. It left a sour taste in my mouth that now after everything he was turning us in.

"He saved you from whoever did that to you?" I ran a hand along my face to mirror the scar that had defiled him. I thought it had been the king who'd one it, but his words proved otherwise. He shot a look my way; anger flickered in his eyes and his brows furrowed. He didn't say anything for a while, and I started to wonder if he was still with me.

"Pascal?"

Startled, he looked around the room, his eyes wide and frantic before settling back into his menacing grin. "Yes, he saved me and granted me the gift of becoming his right-hand-man. I live to serve."

It was hard to believe that a tyrant king such as Roland would save someone like Pascal. Not unless he already knew what kind of powers

Pascal possessed.

It also had me curious about whether or not Pascal had ever been shown kindness or if anyone had ever asked him what it was *he* wanted. Had he ever been shown a world besides the darkness he lived within? By the sounds of it, he'd only done what he was told to do and nothing more. By the scars on his face, there was no doubt the torture he'd been subjected to was terrible and wrong. A tinge of sorrow built in my chest.

"So that's it, all of this was for nothing?"

Pascal threw his head back and laughed. "Of course not, everything will work out as it's intended to. It always does, little dove. Now, I suggest you get yourself comfortable, it's going to be a long ride."

Pascal let out a whistle and the door flew open. A kingsman approached. The way Pascal's eyes darted from me to the kingsman, there was a scared boy behind those eyes, and I just had to figure out how to get through to him. He was a powerful wizard, and I may be the only one with the means to get him to see reason.

I pressed a hand on top of the desk, unsure if what I was about to say would change anything, but I had to try. "I know what it's like to answer to someone, that sense of duty is what keeps some of us grounded in this life. You have to do what you need to, and I respect that. I hope that you know what you're doing. Just know, Pascal, that I forgive you."

I didn't, not exactly, but his look of shock was exactly what I'd been hoping for.

We were going to escape Khan and Pascal was going to be the one to get us out.

A KING'S REVENGE

KING ROLAND SAT ON HIS THRONE, FINGERS DRUMMING against the arms as his eyes bored into me. His hatred seemed to grow by the second. He'd been silent since Hook and I had been brought in. The rest of the crew were sent to the cells beneath the castle. We knelt before him for so long that my legs had gone numb.

I wasn't sure what we were waiting for, but the itch to get to Frankie worsened with each passing minute. Fire danced in the king's eyes. His lips pursed and brows furrowed. He looked worse than he had when I first sat in this room. His hair was disheveled, his tired eyes sported dark circles, and there was an odd odor rolling off him like he hadn't bathed since our last encounter.

After several minutes of agonizing silence, the door to my right opened and a kingsman strode in. Every muscle tensed and my jaw clenched as I recognized those dark eyes and crooked nose. This was the man who'd hurt Frankie.

"Kristof," the king deadpanned, "were you successful?"

Kristof shook his head. "Sorry, your Majesty, it appears he is invoking a code of silence."

King Roland slammed his fast against the arm of his throne before glaring at me. "*You*. What did you do to my wizard?"

What did *I* do? Pascal was the one who'd brought me here. He was fine when I'd left him, though he'd acted strangely when we were taken from King Roland's ship. He kept glancing at me and rubbing his face. He'd left with who I now knew as Kristof and winked at me. I'd chalked it up to him being his weird self. His creepy gestures had grown on me a bit during our time together on the *Betty*, but this felt slightly different. Though it was surprising that he was remaining quiet. I figured he would have at least told the king about the trident.

"I'm not sure what you mean—"

"You know *damn* well what I mean," the king spat. "I thought sending him off to watch you was the only way to ensure you'd do as you were told. Now, my strongest weapon is refusing to tell us anything about your journey. What kind of lies did you spew? What spells did you place on my wizard, witch?"

"She did nothing—"

"Mind your tongue, Hook. I don't need to remind you of who I have below this very floor, do I?"

Beside me, Hook shook, fighting against the shackles holding his hands behind his back.

"King Roland," I said before Hook could say something he'd regret, "I swear I did nothing to Pascal. He was a nuisance, and I ignored him the entire time he was on my vessel. If he's not speaking to you, then maybe it is you who did something."

A hand shot out across my face, and I tasted blood. Kristof towered over me and I spat, glaring at the kingsman. I'd made a promise to kill this man when he'd hurt Frankie, and I was going to hold onto that promise. That would be the one and only time he'd strike me. If I got out of this alive, I'd show him Slayer's wrath. If I ever got it back. They'd taken it and the rest of our weapons. Yet again, I felt naked without it.

"Kristof, take Pascal to the chamber. See to it that you remind him of who he is and who he serves."

The kingsman's lips curled into a wide grin. "With pleasure, your Majesty."

I tried to not show the worry on my face. Why in sea's sake was Pascal not saying anything? Sure, he'd risked his life for me on more than one occasion, but this just seemed reckless and stupid. All he had to do was tell the king that we were on track. The Leviathan would be dead and the cargo back in his possession soon. None of this made a lick of sense. Unless he knew something I didn't. I needed to know why he was doing this, and to save him from whatever King Roland was going to do to him. I don't know why, but something in the back of my mind screamed at me to help him.

Hold on, Pascal, I'm coming for you.

"Onto other matters," King Roland stood from his throne and approached us.

"King Roland, I know where the Leviathan is. If you just give us a few extra days, a week at most, I will have the Leviathan's head at your feet. There was no cargo in its cave, but I promise I will kill the beast for you. If only you—"

"Silence, witch! I don't care about a stupid beast."

My brow furrowed as I looked at Hook who shrugged. "Then why are we here?"

"Now that's the right question to ask." King Roland placed his hands behind his back and rocked on his heels. "Daughter of Ursa."

My stomach dropped. He *knew*? How was that possible? I hadn't even known Ursa was my mother until a few days ago. Pascal hadn't said anything, so where had he got this information from? The idea that I'd been betrayed came to mind, but everyone in my crew was loyal to me. Unless it was one of Hook's men. I kept my eyes locked on the king, hoping I was wrong.

"You know she's Ursa's daughter, how?" Hook asked the question for me, for which I was grateful.

"Of course I know." The king's lips pulled into a smug smile. "Ursa told me the first time we met. Who do you think brought her sister to me?"

I surged forward, but someone grabbed my shoulders, pinning me in place. I'd completely forgotten that a row of kingsmen stood behind us, weapons at the ready in case I tried to use my gift.

Ursa had orchestrated this entire thing. How far did her ruse go? How could I have been so stupid? I'd fallen right in line with her plan, one I didn't even know was brewing.

Another thought rushed to the forefront of my mind, and I blinked back the tears. I'd considered Ursa's involvement in my fathers' deaths before, but this all but solidified it. They'd taken me from her and hid me away for years. Maybe she found out where I was and sent someone to get me back. It still didn't answer why they didn't stay behind and wait for me to return. Either way, it was going to be the first thing I asked her before I shoved my dagger in her cold, black heart. My entire body shook with unrelenting rage as King Roland continued.

"She and I had a deal. All I had to do was hold on to your sister and force you in the right direction. In return I'd get power, land, and the chance to rule a kingdom below the sea."

I couldn't stop the laugh that flew out of my mouth. "She promised you Atlantis?"

He lowered himself until he was inches from my face. "Laugh at me one more time and I will gladly slit your throat here and now." He took a step back. "She promised me glory, and I was all ready to receive that when she showed up demanding I hand over your sister." King Roland began pacing, voice rising to a shout. "I did as she asked, thinking she'd hold up her end of the deal. But she laughed in my face—"

I stopped listening. I didn't give a damn about what he spewed. All I could focus on was the dread that washed over me.

Ursa has Frankie.

I wanted to rip through these chains and kill every person in this room.

I kept my head lowered, trying to keep my burning hatred to myself as King Roland continued to throw his tantrum, ranting and raving.

Hook said my name, but my mind was overloading. Frankie wasn't here. I had to find her. I had to get her back. She didn't deserve any of this and yet because she was my sister, because she was part of my life, she was being held hostage. Again.

How was I going to fix this? The trident was still around my neck, but with my hands at my back there was nothing I could do. The cuffs, to my surprise, weren't iron, but I supposed with the several guards behind me, iron wasn't necessary. Either that or the king had lost his mind. Though, if I even attempted to use my magic, the guards would act. I had to stay calm, Frankie needed me more than ever right now.

"—which is why I've decided to take matters into my own hands and end your life."

"What?" I snarled, "What good will that do? Ursa will just hunt you down."

"I have a plan, but you don't need to worry yourself with that." King Roland stood before Hook. "*You* are free to go. Clayton has found a way to pay his debt and will be released. A few of my men will escort you and what remains of your crew back to the docks. I've instructed them to watch you get on Arie's ship and depart before they return to the castle."

Hook stilled beside me, his gaze flicking from the king to me. I knew he was only here for his brother and now he had the means to go, but the look of conflict on his face said he was ready to protest. I wouldn't give him the opportunity to do so. Hook had been a great ally and now he had the means to get out and be free.

"I won't—"

"Good," I said, interrupting Hook as I kept my eyes pointed at the king, "he's been nothing but trouble since I saved his ass, anyway. I hope you rot out there."

Hook shot me a look that I ignored. I didn't have time to feel bad or acknowledge the hurt I imagined was on his face. I needed King Roland to believe that I still despised this man. If Hook was getting out, I'd ensure the king had no reason to keep him here.

"Let me have Arie's crew," said Hook. "They aren't a part of this, and I'll need more men to man the ship. They know it better than I do, anyway."

My heart swelled. Even though I'd just dismissed him, he was trying to save my crew. A part of me felt sorry for hurting him, but it was necessary, and I knew he would understand. Or so I hoped.

King Roland mulled over Hook's words. "Fine, I only need Arie. Once Ursa hears what I've done, all this will be over anyway. I'll have killed two sea witches and the glory will be all mine."

I kept my eyes on the stone floor, refusing to watch Hook leave as I waited for what came next. If King Roland planned to kill me now, I'd be done for, but he was someone who enjoyed flaunting his kills, so I hoped he'd create some sort of spectacle first. Getting time to think things through clearly was goal number one. From there I'd come up with a solid plan.

"Daniel, take Arie downstairs. Let her enjoy her last few hours alive in the dungeons with the rest of the sewer rats."

Thank the gods. I'd been down in those cells before, iron coated the room I'd surely be locked in. I was going to have to get crafty if I was going to make it out of this mess.

"You think you've won," I sneered, "but you have no idea what you're up against. Ursa will kill you, and if she doesn't? I will."

King Roland's brow rose. "It'll be hard to kill me when you're already dead."

The guard I presumed to be Daniel, stood in front of me. His golden-brown skin and blue eyes were an odd, yet beautiful match. With ease, he lifted me up and threw me over his shoulder before stepping out of the room.

"I can walk, you know." I squirmed, but Daniel held firm, his arms tightening around me, and I fought to breathe.

Not until we were far away from the throne room did he set me down. He ignored me and nudged me forward.

We walked along hallways and down several staircases until arriving at the cell I'd occupied last time I was here. Daniel shoved me forward before locking the door behind me.

"You're a fighter, I like that. Seeing you handle yourself against the king, it takes balls. I've heard of the things you've done and the monsters you've slain. If we'd met in different circumstances, I may have actually liked you."

I whirled around and shot him a glare. "If that's the case then let me go."

Daniel smirked. "I did say under different circumstances. But, nice try, that's not going to work on me. I am loyal only to the king. I live to serve."

I gawked at him. Pascal had said the exact same thing. It was as if they were all brainwashed to believe the same rubbish. What did King Roland do to deserve this kind of loyalty? A king who had burned a family alive inside a barn because they refused to pay his outrageous taxes. A man said to have sent his own son to the mining fields when he refused to become a kingsman. How could anyone stand by someone who did that?

So why did Pascal? He'd said the king saved him, but what did that mean? If the king was fine throwing away his only child, what made Pascal so important?

A part of me knew he'd enjoyed his time on the *Betty*. He'd been weird and wild and yet had managed to grow on me. I didn't think he felt the same. Not unless this was all a trick. A nagging voice in the back of my head still said to be careful.

I slid onto the cold stone, darkness looming over me as Daniel's footsteps faded. A draft whistled through the brick walls, and I let out a lengthy breath. I needed to come up with a plan.

Time had ceased to exist for all I knew. I'd lost track of it rotting away in this damn cell. The draft grew colder, indicating that night was upon me. One of the servants had brought me food; a bowl of soup and stale bread. I ate it, keeping my energy and strength as best I could. Other than that, it was quiet. Too quiet.

My mind lingered on the thought of what Ursa could be doing to

Frankie as I lay in this cell. Was she being tortured? Was Ursa filling her head with lies, telling her that I'd never come back? Or that I was as good as dead? I tried to push those thoughts away, but they were relentless. At every turn, I continued to fail Frankie. This couldn't be the end.

Leaning my head back against the wall, I still didn't have a concrete plan. My best option so far was waiting until a kingsman arrived to take me back upstairs. Once away from these bars, I'd reveal the trident. There was a high chance that I'd be forced to fight my way out of here. I'd rather go down with a fight than be beheaded by Guilly. My options were limited, and not great, but it was all I had. I just had to—

The shuffling of feet pulled me from my thoughts. Muffled voices echoed off the walls as two figures approached. A blinding light guided them toward me. I shielded my eyes from the lantern and did my best to peek through my fingers. "Pascal?"

"Hey, little dove."

It was difficult to see his face in the dim light, but what I did see had my eyes widening. His good eye was swollen shut and a gash on his lip dripped blood down his chin.

Kristof appeared next to him. "Looks like you'll get some company after all."

"What did you do to him?" I snapped, rushing over to try and get a better look at him, but Kristof opened the cell next to mine and pushed Pascal inside. He slipped into the shadows beyond the wall that separated us.

"Why do you care?" Kristof narrowed his eyes and I backed away, clearing my throat.

"I don't."

Keys rattled as Kristof locked Pascal's cell. Slipping them back into his pocket, he stepped over to mine. Specks of blood covered his coat and the hands he curled around the bars were scraped and crimson. He'd tortured and beaten Pascal.

This only further proved that King Roland was a despicable human being who never got his own hands dirty. To hurt the one person who had done all that work for him, who killed his enemies and helped further his rise to the throne… I knew of Pascal's transgressions, he wasn't innocent, but he had been trying. Hells, he could have killed Nathaniel back in the Ugly Duckling, but he hadn't. If that didn't show his potential to be a decent human being, I didn't know what would. Looking at Kristof, I realized the king would always stoop to the lowest level.

The lantern flickered as he lowered it to his belt. When his hand rose again, he held a knife—no, a dagger. My hands balled into fists at my side and I bit my cheek to keep from speaking. My eyes were unable to pull from what he held.

Slayer.

"You know, it's a pity that this fine piece of weaponry was being wasted on a witch. But I look forward to the next person I get to torture with it."

I clamped my mouth shut from dropping. He'd tortured Pascal with *my* blade.

A whimper echoed through the cell next to me as I searched for restraint. Kristof would get what was coming to him. He may have

Slayer, but he wouldn't for long. And when I got it back, I'd happily lodge it in his chest.

Once the kingsman disappeared into the shadows, I scurried over to the wall, wishing it wasn't blocking me from seeing Pascal.

"Pascal, are you all right?"

"Failed, I did. Me. Why?"

I rubbed a hand over my face, trying to keep my voice from cracking. He sounded so weak, his words breathless and layered with pain. He wasn't making much sense, everything grew jumbled the more he spoke. I didn't know what they'd done to him, but I had to pull him together. We were going to need each other if we wanted to escape.

"You didn't fail anyone, Pascal. You did a good thing, something done by a person with a good soul."

A snarl rang out and something pounded against the wall on Pascal's side. "Why would I help you? No, wait, I *wanted* to... but why? Something... something's not right with my head."

"Pascal," I pleaded. "Nothing is wrong with you. You risked your life for someone else, that's what good people do. Nothing about what you did was wrong. You don't deserve to be treated that way and I promise I won't let them hurt you again." I paused and silence grew as well as my nerves, was he still with me? "Do you hear me, Pascal? You're a part of my crew now. We sacrifice for each other. You and I are getting out of here, but I need your help to do so."

When he said nothing, I lowered myself to the floor. The necklace around my neck reminded me that I had a weapon still at my disposal. I wasn't sure if mermaid magic worked against...

I shot up to my feet as I rushed to the bars. Why in sea's sake didn't I notice this before? There was no burn, no sting or bite from the iron that I knew this cell was made from. I should be sitting as far away from them as I could get, feeling my magic weaken. Yet, I felt nothing. How was that possible? Unless the king decided to place me in another cell, but this was the same one down to the very stone I'd used to carve etchings into the brick just weeks ago.

"Pascal, why is the iron not harming me?" I wasn't sure that he would answer, but it was worth a shot.

It was a few minutes before he said, "Sea witches. Mermaids. Different blood, different magic."

Deciding to put my theory to the test, I inched my hand forward and wrapped my hand around the bar. Nothing happened. *Hells*. I guess opening myself up to new magic came with all sorts of fun perks. If I could blast through these bars, Pascal and I could get out of here.

Stepping away, I took the necklace from around my neck. I held it out, searching my inner self for the magic I'd only just begun to understand, drawing it from within. A blue-green light left my fingers to swirl around the necklace and in a blink, the trident appeared in my grasp. It appeared heavy and tough to wield, but in my hands, it was light and twirled through the air with ease. Feeling confident enough, I pointed it at the lock. My heart raced as I opened my awareness and let the trident work its magic.

Please let this work.

The magic built in my hands, sliding down my fingers and through the trident so fast, I barely saw it leave the prongs. It struck the lock, melting it, and the door swung open. Relief washed over me as I raced to Pascal's cell. He sat in the far corner, his arms wrapped around his legs and he rocked back and forth.

I was drawn to his sorrow, an ache suffering in my chest as I used the trident to open his cell. Slowly, I approached him and lowered myself until my face was level with his. It took him time to focus on me but once he did, the grin I'd grown accustomed to lit up his face.

Kneeling this close to him, his features were more visible, as well as the damage that Kristof had inflicted. Not only was his face bruised, but his clothes were tattered and shredded. Dry blood coated his trousers and shirt, and there was a gash on his leg that must have been responsible for his limp.

"Little dove, what can I do for you?"

"I'd like to get you out of here. Will you come with me?"

"N-no, he'll kill me." He scurried away from me and his voice shook worse than his hands. "I-I belong here. With the rats. I live to serve... I live to... I..."

His voice trailed off and I placed a hand upon his. He regarded me with narrowed eyes, but I refused to pull away. "You live to be your own person. If you come with me, you can have whatever you want, be whoever you want. Pascal let's get out of here and show these bastards what two powerful people can do. Let's take down Ursa and prove to the world we're forces to be reckoned with."

Pascal considered me, eyes fluttering from my hand to my face and back again. "You're a good captain, and an even better person than I could ever be. I don't deserve your kindness."

His mental state was like the waves of the sea, constantly changing. Yet, if I could wield the sea, maybe I could help a wizard control his brain again.

"You helped me when you didn't have to. It's time I returned the favor. Now, let's get out of here before any of the guards show up. It's already becoming suspicious that none have started patrolling through here yet." I stood, holding my hand out to Pascal who took it and rose. I tried to give him my arm for support, but he pushed it away.

"First thing's first, how about we go visit a certain kingsman?"

Pascal trembled, his hands curled into fists as he took in a deep breath. He gestured toward the exit. "After you, *captain*."

Using as much stealth as we could, Pascal showed me to Kristof's room. It was late, so I was hoping he would be asleep. I didn't exactly know what to expect going into this. This man hit my sister and tortured Pascal with Slayer. Every fiber of my soul wanted to rip into him until there was nothing left.

We stopped in front of a small wooden door, soft voices mumbled beyond it, and I stilled. Who could be in there with him? Not caring who was beyond the door, I kicked it open. Two bodies scurried out from underneath the bed sheets, the small lantern on the table letting us see that a woman joined him in his bed. I recognized her as one of the servants who brought me food while down in the cells.

"What the—" Kristof rolled out of bed and drew his pistol from the side table. He whipped around and pointed the gun at me. My throat tightened. *Hells*, I should have known this guy would sleep with his weapon close. I closed my eyes, waiting for death that never came.

Opening my eyes, my jaw dropped as my eyes darted from Pascal to Kristof. Pascal had the guard by the throat and pressed against the wall.

"Now, Kristof, play nice. We've only come to have a nice little chat."

Kristof winced and slowly lowered his gun. His eyes bored into mine as the woman next to him shook.

"Leave, and don't come back." I bit out. "Oh, and if you say one word about this, I'll pay you a visit next." I gestured toward the door and she leapt out of bed. I'd never seen someone get dressed and run from a room as fast as she did.

I turned and stepped closer to Kristof.

"Where is it?" I demanded. "Where is my dagger?"

Pascal let go but stayed where he was. "All of this for a stupid dagger?" Kristof laughed, pointing to his belt where Slayer lay. I picked it up and put it back where it belonged, feeling whole once again. "You won't get out of here alive. The second you step out these doors, they'll come for you."

I chuckled. "Oh, I don't think I'll have a problem with that. Who would tell them, after all?"

Kristof narrowed his eyes. "You plan on killing me, hunter?"

I lowered the trident, stepping away from the bed and shook my head. "As much as I would love to cut you open and set fire to your entrails, I'm not a monster."

Plus, when King Roland heard about our escape, Kristof would be the one he'd go to for answers. After all, he was the last one to see us.

"No, you're just a worthless piece of garbage. Poor Captain Arie, can't even save her own sister from–"

Pascal shot forward, his hands curling around Kristof's throat. He muttered under his breath, eyes wild. I knew that look and if I didn't stop this now, I wasn't sure I'd be able to stop him from doing something he may regret. To my surprise, Pascal let go of his own accord and stepped back.

"Apologize to the lady."

"What?"

"I said," Pascal shoved his fist into Kristof's stomach. "*Apologize.*"

Kristof coughed and shifted to look at me. "I'll never apologize to a cu—"

A ball of light hurled from Pascal's palm, hitting Kristof in the chest. He sank to the floor as blood pooled around him.

Shit. "Pascal, we have to go."

"Not before I—"

"Leave him be, he's not worth it. One day he will get what's coming to him, but right now we need to get down to the docks."

Several seconds passed before Pascal moved away from the guard. His face was void of emotion as he strode to the open window. "We leave through here."

I nodded and leapt out the window after him. We ran through the streets of Khan until the docks appeared and found my men standing over several groaning and unconscious kingsmen.

"Arie!" shouted Keenan, who slammed into me, wrapping his arms around me so tightly my breath caught in my throat.

"O-okay, y-yes I'm f-fine."

He pulled back and smirked. "Of course you are. What's he

doing here?"

Pascal shot Keenan a look, but I stood between them. "He's here because he deserves to be. Now let's get the hell out of here while we still can."

"We were just coming to get you, but we were a little occupied," Hook said as he approached. I peered around him to find more kingsmen unconscious along the dock. The rest of the crew stood at attention, ready to storm the castle to save me. My chest ached with their loyalty, and I blinked back the tears that threatened to spill down my cheeks.

"Thank you, all. I'd love to give a proper speech, but it won't take long for—"

Bells sounded from the castle that had my crew running to the ship. It was time to face the one who had started all this. The witch who had cast a plague over anything she touched. I vowed to put an end to it.

Because I wasn't just a pirate. I was a hunter, a witch of the sea, and tonight I would prove to the fiercest monster in existence that I was *not* someone to be trifled with.

XIV. UNFORTUNATE SOULS

"YOU'D RATHER TAKE PASCAL WITH YOU THAN ME?" Hook's red-hot stare wasn't going to change the fact I needed Pascal for this mission. Hook was a formidable ally, of course, but Pascal's skills were designed for this kind of monster. Ursa—the Leviathan—was dangerous and full of magic. There was no telling what kind of tricks she had up her sleeve. Pascal and I would head to Ursa's Island by using the last two pearls she'd given me. He hadn't been happy when I'd told him as we left port. We'd barely managed to get away before cannon fire was upon us. King Roland would search the seas for us in no time, but right now we had a worse opponent to fight. Hook knew what we were going up against and wanted in on the action. I understood that and respected it, but I was still captain of the *Betty* and if he wanted to stay on board he was going to have to come to terms with that.

There was also the fact that I didn't exactly trust Pascal's current state at that moment. He still muttered and spoke in riddles half the time, and when he wasn't, he'd asked to help. Sometimes too eagerly. One moment he was attacking Sanders who was trying to tend to his wounds, and the next laughing with Hector and Nathaniel about gods knew what. Leaving him here without me to stand in the way would put everyone in danger.

"I've already explained this, Hook. Pascal knows just as much as you do about the Leviathan, if not more. I need him to help weaken her or at the very least keep her at bay. I'll need you to take the crew and sail to her island. I'll create the winds to help push *Black Betty* along and you'll be there before you know it."

Hook blew out his cheeks, raking his fingers through his hair as we leaned against the ship's railing. It had been a couple of days since escaping Khan and Ursa's Island wasn't too far away now. Hook, Keenan, Pascal, and I had spent one of those days coming up with a game plan. One that only myself and Pascal liked.

We were to find Ursa and Frankie first. The crew would ready themselves out on the water in case Ursa decided to change into the Leviathan. Keeping the fight contained to the island and in human forms, that was key. Not that I thought we wouldn't be able to take down the beast, but I didn't want lives lost today.

"How are you so sure you can trust him?" Hook asked, turning his head toward Pascal who sat cross-legged on a barrel a few feet from us.

"In his current state, I don't. But this way I can keep an eye on him and ensure he doesn't do anything he will regret when his mind is stable again. I can handle him. You just have to trust *me*." I was done with this discussion and settled on something a little more personal. "How's Clayton?"

Hook waited a few minutes, probably contemplating whether or not to accept my change in subject. Finally, he turned to me and huffed. "Stupid is how he is. He still won't tell me how he paid off his debt, but I'm just glad he's okay."

"I'm happy you have your brother back."

Thinking about Clayton and Hook made me realize how much I missed Frankie, and how stupid I was to leave her behind all those years ago. Having her on this ship at her age wasn't exactly the right move, but I should have tried harder to include her in the decision, to at least make her see that everything was going to be okay. Even so, I had no right to abandon her. I was her only family and I hadn't returned when I should have. Now, I'd spend the rest of my life trying to make it up to her.

Hook placed a hand on my shoulder, his touch settling deep within me. I welcomed it, even if I shouldn't have. I turned to him, our eyes locking as heat wrapped itself around me.

"We'll get her back."

I nodded. Above, the clouds I'd been waiting for finally rolled in. I could have pulled them to me, but we still had a ways to go and I wasn't in a rush. Sure, I needed to get to Frankie, but the smart move was to ensure we were ready. I couldn't go after Ursa unprepared.

"It's time. Are you ready for this?" I asked.

"Can anyone really be ready to go up against a man-eating, witch-beast?"

He had a point, but I let it go and ventured over to Pascal. Rather than ask if he was okay when I already had a hunch that he wasn't, I collected a pearl from my pocket and held it out for him.

"Are you sure you want *my* help? I was the one who kidnapped your sister to begin with, remember?"

"Which is why you can help me get her back. Think of it as a way to redeem yourself."

The two of us had gone over this plenty of times. He was a misfit, a wizard who did terrible things but was trying to do better, to be better. I still wasn't sure what had caused the change in him, maybe in due time he would tell me. Even someone as messed up as Pascal needed a little care. I'd taken on many men with troubled pasts. Men who'd killed, who'd spent their lives fighting to survive. Pascal belonged with us and as long as I was captain of this ship, that wouldn't change.

"All right, little dove, if you say so."

I clutched the pearl in my hand and stepped away from him so he could climb down next to me. Smith and Keenan joined us, followed by Hector and Nathaniel; most of the other members were busy readying the ship.

"I'm going to make this short and sweet. Everyone knows their role and what to do. When Pascal and I leave, the battle begins and it doesn't stop until Ursa is dead. Stay safe."

"Good luck," Smith called, his hand held out. "Things have been interesting since coming aboard the *Betty*. Those of us from the

Marauder weren't sure about you when we first arrived, but it's obvious you care more about the people on your crew than anyone else. I respect that, and so does Hook even if he doesn't admit it."

I laughed and shook Smith's hand, ignoring the glare Hook gave his first mate. "Thank you, Smith."

I took a step back to stand next to Pascal. The pearl in my hand pulsed with magic as I tossed it to the floor. Pascal followed suit, leaving the crew and *Black Betty* behind.

We landed rather abruptly on the sandy beach of Ursa's island. The sea was at our backs as I stood, dusting off the sand and searching our surroundings. With the pearls being Ursa's magic, I wouldn't put it past her to know we were here.

Something inside attempted to pull me further down the beach, as if Ursa were calling me to her. For all I knew, she was. Which meant she was far closer to the sea than I would have liked, but it didn't change my plan.

"Pascal, are you going to be able to do this? We can go after her together if you—"

"I'm going to clean up my mess. I've got this." Pascal nodded before heading off toward the forest.

Ominous thoughts squirmed in the back of my mind and no matter how hard I tried, they refused to cease. Pascal would oversee getting my sister free from Ursa's clutches. He'd hide in the trees until

I gave the signal. With Ursa distracted, he'd have the opportunity to grab her and take off. We didn't have any more portal pearls, but Pascal assured me he could handle it and I tried to not question him. Though it was hard when he was in charge of protecting my baby sister. I had almost changed my mind about taking Hook, but the look and need in Pascal's eyes to right his wrongs had overpowered that thought.

Walking along the beach, the hum of the sea brightened into a familiar melody. The song soothed me as I trudged forward. I didn't understand who'd spoken to me after opening my mermaid magic, but I knew every time I heard the music that I wasn't alone.

Grateful to be heading toward Ursa with the sea on my side, I rounded a bend to find Ursa standing on the beach in a hue of purple glow. It hovered like a thick fog that surrounded both her and Frankie. I gasped and leapt behind a rock. My heart wanted to rip through my ribcage at the sight of my sister. Peeking around the rock, I cursed. Frankie floated above the water just off the shore, unmoving as Ursa spoke in a foreign tongue.

I searched the area for her minions, Klaus and Stephan, but they were nowhere to be found. Hopefully Pascal wouldn't run into them either. Surrounding Ursa along the sand were several stones surrounded by the same purple glow. It was almost as though she was feeding her magic into the stones and back to her.

"You can stop hiding, daughter, I know you are there," Ursa called out, stepping out from the circle that kept the magic flowing.

"Give her back," I demanded as I left the shield of the rock. "Now."

Ursa threw her head back and laughed. "Oh, dear child, you don't think it's going to be that easy, do you? Though, it could be if you hand over that." She pointed to her neck indicating the trident that hung around my own.

"I don't understand, why did you take her?"

Ursa's smile grew. "You were trying to locate your sister and I wanted the trident. Now both of us get what we want. All you need to do is hand over the trident and I will release your sister."

There was no chance in hell I'd do that. "The deal was that you'd help me find the Leviathan if I brought you the Trident. I said nothing about my sister, but you knew that. After all, you're the one who told King Roland where to find her in the first place."

Ursa's smile faltered and then faded. "Sounds like you know everything, best to end this now then so that—"

"So, you can steal my magic and kill me?" I snapped, taking a few steps closer. I had to do my best to keep her facing me and away from Frankie.

Ursa's lips pursed. "Do you really need it? What good is the gift of mermaid magic when you have no plans of sitting on Atlantis's throne?"

While that rang true, it didn't mean she needed to know that. "I don't know where you got that information, but I promise you, you have no idea what my plans are."

"Well, you certainly won't find the one who murdered your fathers by sitting on a throne now, will you? Surely that's more important."

My muscles tensed and jaw clenched at her words. "I already have, and she just happens to be standing before me."

"Me?" Ursa doubled over in laughter once more. "You actually think *I* killed them? Oh, how I wish that were true. I'd love to take their souls and add them to my collection. The souls of mermaids are so much more potent than those of mundane humans."

She expected me to believe she had nothing to do with their deaths. After setting this entire thing in motion, she had to at least know something. "If not you, then who?"

"You may want to ask the Elders of the Brotherhood. Though I must admit, whoever did it deserves to live a long happy life for their good deed. Those mermen kept you from me and got what was coming to them. Now, be a good little daughter and give me what I want. I've had enough of this chatter."

Anger continued to build inside as I drew on my magic. The sky above was already covered in dark clouds and the waves grew restless under Frankie. I was running out of time. Where was Pascal?

"Release Frankie."

A strike of lightning hit the ground between us, and I cried out as the ground beneath me quaked, sending a shock through my body. Ursa remained where she was, unwavering from the lightning's force. I wanted to lash out at the gods just then for giving me a mother who'd rather kill me than teach me how to wield magic as she did. She'd moved so fast and without warning. I had to spend time letting mine build.

"Your demands are futile, I am the power here, not you. I will take the trident from your cold, dead body if I must. Of course, after I drain your magic completely."

"How could someone want to kill their own daughter? Did you ever actually care about me?" Words poured from my mouth so fast I had no time to filter them. All the pent-up rage I never realized I had spilled out. "You'd sacrifice your own daughter for what... power?"

"Witches *are* power, child. They are, at their core, the very essence of greatness. All you have to do is be willing to give up your soul. As far as you are concerned, your power is" —Ursa sniffed the air in front of her—"more than I could have ever imagined. I thought siphoning it from you as a baby would give me its rawest form. Now I see I was wrong. Consuming souls is one thing, but having the power of two sea witches would make me unstoppable."

She really would have killed her own child. A small part of me had hoped Rylan was wrong, that she would never take my power and end my life. Yet here she was, ready to do it again. The second she got her hands on this trident it would all be over. I knew what she was but hearing her admit it sent my stomach into knots.

"So, it's true, you are the Leviathan. You're taking the souls of people."

"You could say that. It's simply a form I take on to collect the souls of willing participants."

"Even though the Leviathan is consuming you and the souls you gather?"

The air between Ursa and I thickened as thunder and lightning assaulted the sky. "My patience with you is growing very thin, daughter. I'll ask you one more time, hand it over or..."

Relief flooded through me as Pascal appeared from behind the trees. He glanced at me and then to Frankie as he crept closer. I held my breath, listening to Ursa go on and on about all the ways she was going to consume my soul and magic and use it to destroy Atlantis. I was trying to keep her attention, but the need to make sure Frankie was safe worsened with each step Pascal took.

"There's nothing you can do, Arie. Not unless you want your sister's death on your hands. Do the right thing and let's end this."

Something popped up from the water, underneath where Frankie levitated. My gaze flickered to it and I could have sworn it was some sort of creature. A second head popped up from the surface and I bit my lip from yelling out. Pascal must have noticed them too because he stopped his advance and glanced at me.

"Rylan has scorned me for the last time. I will take over Atlantis and there is nothing anyone—"

Ursa narrowed her eyes on me. I'd been doing a good job of keeping my focus on her, but something came and went on her face. "I see that you've brought back up. How pathetic. Stephan, Klaus, take care of him for me while I deal with my *daughter*."

The two figures in the water moved closer to shore, their snake-like bodies grew in size and limbs emerged from their smooth skin. Were those serpents? Shapeshifting serpents, to be exact. Stephan and Klaus stepped from the water and blocked Pascal's path. I had to trust that Pascal could handle himself and focused on Ursa.

I removed the necklace, calling on my power as the trident came to life. Just as it appeared, a blinding light assaulted my vision, sending the weapon to the sand as I clutched my burning eyes. I hissed and fell to my knees as I searched for the trident. My fingers sifted through the sand until I found it close by and returned to my feet. My vision was slowly returning and all I could make out was Pascal and Ursa's minions attacking one another.

No, there was something else, too. Muffled groans followed by a wet sloshing sound, I still couldn't see much as I turned, trying to work out the direction of the noises when something wrapped itself around my ankle.

Crying out, I thrashed against what held me, but it was no use. It dragged me across the sand. I did my best to turn and see what had me, only to find the Leviathan's full form. No. My *mother's* form. Her snake-like body was covered in glistening scales that cascaded down her curved frame. Long tentacles slapped against the sandy beach. They stretched almost twenty feet each and were dark as the night sky. Hundreds of suction cups covered the underside and oozed with a green substance. What in sea's sake was that? The smell of burning flesh and rotting seaweed assaulted my nostrils as the tentacle tightened its grasp. Unrelenting pain surged through my leg as the Leviathan continued to drag me toward the sea.

I followed the scales up to find a pair of beady violet eyes boring into me. The monster's long face narrowed to a snout with two slitted nostrils. Below that, a set of jagged teeth snapped the air.

I had to get this thing off me before it reached the water. Seizing the trident, I stabbed the tentacle that held me. Ursa screeched and let go. I rolled to my feet and ignored the pain in my leg. Taking a deep breath, I centered myself and opened my awareness to the storm that loomed above. If she wanted to take this to the sea then so be it. The sea gave the Leviathan an advantage, but I had one too.

The surface of the water came to an eerie stillness as I waited for her next attack. My stomach clenched. The *Betty* wasn't here yet and Pascal was busy fighting the shifters. I was alone. My feet touched the water and I hissed at the cold. Gills formed along my neck as water swirled around me, and built, lifting me into its funnel.

A tentacle broke the surface, followed by three more before Ursa's head shot out.

A voice rang inside my mind.

She's strong, but you've got the magic of a thousand kings running through your veins. The trident is your best weapon here. Use it and remember that there are more than just your crew who can aid you.

The woman's voice I'd heard before came and went, giving me a sliver of hope.

Ursa swam back and forth. I had to make the first move. As fast as my reflexes allowed, I pushed the trident forward like a spear. Blue lightning shot out, but she was quicker. She launched herself up and out of the water. Her body slammed onto the surface, sending a giant wave hurtling toward me.

I barely had time to dive below the water before it hit. I kicked, guiding myself back to the surface when one of her tentacles wrapped around my middle, lifting me into the air. Flames flickered in the back of Ursa's throat and flecks of ash left her nostrils. My eyes widened. Hells, she could breathe fire?

Shit. It was bad enough that Ursa had the powers of a sea witch, but now on top of that, I had to kill a fire-breathing, sea witch with tentacles. My odds at victory were lowering by the second.

I brought the prongs of the trident down on the tentacle that held me, causing her to let go just as flames scorched the air around me. I plummeted to the water and Ursa toppled sideways, crashing into the sea like a whale breaching.

Her force pulled me under. I kicked my tail as hard as I could and tried to hold onto the trident, although the drag was so strong, it was nearly impossible.

Ready to surrender? Another voice sounded in my mind, this time it resembled Ursa's, only much deeper and grainier. I fought against her hold, ignoring her as my mind raced. My heart thudded harder than it ever had before.

Just then, a shadow blocked the light overhead and a wave of relief came over me. *Black Betty.* It had to be my crew… and Hook. I suppressed the flutters that attacked my stomach and prayed to the gods that I was right.

Harpoons broke the surface first, piercing through Ursa's thick scales, but it wasn't enough. She grabbed me again and rose from the surface. I caught a glimpse the *Betty. Thank the gods.* Horror-stricken faces bore into me as I was dragged back into the sea, the Leviathan narrowly missing my ship.

She plunged deeper, far out of the harpoon's reach. The trident slipped, almost falling from my grasp. The pressure of the sea grew as the Leviathan turned to face me once again. Its sharp, jagged teeth snapped. Desperation etched its way into every crease as I kicked, rolling into a somersault. When that huge mouth opened again, I tightened my grip on the trident and thrust. The prongs darted up into her mouth, piercing the flesh. Black liquid seeped from the wound like ink from a squid.

Once again the beast shrieked, though this time it didn't drop me. The tentacle around me tightened, crushing me in its grasp as I fought to breathe. My vision blurred as I kicked and screamed. This couldn't be it. I wasn't going to go out like this. I just got Frankie back, she still needed me and as much as I hated to admit it, I needed her too. We'd come so far and been through too much to not be reunited the right way. She had to know I loved her, that I'd never leave her again no matter who stood in our way. We were going to find the one responsible for our fathers' killer together. No, I wasn't dying today. I closed my eyes and drove the trident into the beast one more time.

One of her tentacles shot out and smacked my legs. Pain rippled through me as my chest ached and lungs burned.

Something brushed against my arm and my eyes shot open to see a small squid latching onto me. *What the hells?* I tried to shake it off, but it held firm. Movement in the distance caught my attention. Hundreds of sea creatures surrounded us. All of their eyes locked onto me; some small and round and others large and bulging. The hairs on my arms rose as they grew closer and my muscles and throat tightened. I'd never seen so many creatures act like this. They waited in the water like an army of men waiting for the command of their leader.

I remembered the first time I'd taken on my mermaid shape and the shark that had helped me move through the sea. It had acted much like they did, swimming and waiting for something to happen. Were they waiting on me? But I had no idea how to command creatures, only how to kill them. Before with the shark, it had done all the work. I didn't tell it what to do.

Ease your mind, Arie. Let the magic of your ancestors guide you.

The voice was right. I was a mermaid, a descendant of the first king of Atlantis, daughter of Rylan and witch of the seas. I could do this.

Once more I opened my awareness and tugged and pulled at the magic I'd come to know as my own. I inhaled and let instinct guide me.

"Attack!" I yelled out, hoping they would understand. The grip around me loosened as hundreds of sea creatures charged at the Leviathan. Biting, stinging, and anything else they could do to get the Leviathan to let go.

The tentacle around me unraveled.

I began to swim away when several of the animals cried out. I whirled around to find that the Leviathan was fighting back. Blinding light slammed against a whale, and then a shark, followed by a stingray. They slumped as life left their body.

Panic surged inside me. What was she doing to them? Was this what it looked like when the beast consumed souls? If that was the case, then I needed to act. The more she consumed, the stronger she'd become.

But how could I defeat her? The woman's voice had told me the trident was at my disposal, but I barely knew how to work it or my mermaid magic. Just like the witch side of me, this was all instinct.

The longer I thought about what to do, the more souls the beast would consume. I pointed the trident at the Leviathan, channeling what energy I could. Maybe all I needed was to strike her down with it. I concentrated, digging deep into my soul, and collecting the magic that had once been hidden from me.

The liquid I'd associated with my mermaid half seemed to fuse with the heat of my witch half. I tried to stop the two from combining, the witch magic surely wouldn't be good to use against someone who was already a witch. As I attempted to rip the different magic apart, the more tangled it became.

Stop fighting.

The voice shouted in my mind, nearly causing me to lose focus.

It wanted me to let the magic come together. Why?

But the voice hadn't steered me wrong yet, so rather than continue to fight against the magic, I let it combine into one perfect ball of energy. I drew it through my bones and muscle, felt it crawl against my skin in a wave of power unlike anything I'd felt before. It consumed every part of me, filling me up until there was no more magic to give.

Again, I pointed the trident at the Leviathan and let it all free.

Blue and purple swirls of light shot from the end, hitting the Leviathan square in its chest. Animals scattered as the beam of magic…

Wait. Why was the beam coming toward me rather than the Leviathan?

I tried to stop, to pull the trident away, but I couldn't move. I cried out as the power ricocheted from the beast back to me. Waves of white orbs left the Leviathan as though the trident was siphoning the souls from her and bringing them to me. Wasn't this what Ursa had planned to do with the trident? I didn't want this, I didn't want to consume the souls. I wanted them to be free.

Then will it so.

As the last orb was sucked into the trident, the beam of light faltered and Ursa screeched out in agony or anger, I wasn't sure. Its long tentacles retracted and the scales turned back to flesh as Ursa's frame returned. Though rather than the porcelain skin and young face I'd come to associate with her, all I saw now was an old woman with wrinkles and sunken eyes that bore into me.

You may have bested me, daughter, but you will not stop her.

Ursa's voice faded. What was she talking about? Stop who? Before I could consider her words, the trident throbbed against my hold. Waves of magic I'd taken in traveled along my skin, soaking into me like a sponge did water.

No. I didn't want this. I closed my eyes once more, knowing that what I was about to do could possibly kill us all. I had no idea what would happen if I released the power without a source for it to enter, but I had no choice. Solidifying that thought in my mind and gathering the last bit of strength I had, I pushed the energy back out.

Light exploded, knocking everything back, careening through the water. I screamed as pain burned me from the inside out. Everything ached and my leg throbbed from where the green ooze had scorched it. Spots danced over my vision and I fought to stay conscious. I caught sight of Ursa who sank into the depths of the sea, still lifeless. Even as the pain continued, I knew that I had won… That even if I died right here and now, everything would be okay. Frankie and I might not have the chance to make amends, or have the opportunity to catch our fathers killer, but I knew she'd be okay. She had to be. Pascal would ensure that Frankie survived. My crew would pick them up and take them wherever they wanted to go.

I took one last breath, my gills stilling as I stopped struggling to stay awake.

XV. GODDESS BLESSED

AWAKEN DESCENDENT OF ATLAS, ARISE AGAIN AS ONE.

The voice surged through me. Breath filled my lungs as I was pulled from a deep slumber. My eyes fluttered open, the light burning.

I blinked away the spots and took in the familiar room. One I shouldn't have been in. Why was I in the infirmary of Atlantis? I should be dead, in Davy Jones's locker along with Ursa. Yet, I wasn't. Beside me someone spoke in excited tones, and I tried to sit up, hissing as pain tore through my ribs. Someone grabbed my shoulder and pushed me back down.

"Easy, you need to rest. The nurses say you're pretty banged up still. Your mermagic is trying to heal you, but it won't work unless you relax." Hook's words cut through my confusion, and I rubbed my eyes.

Hook, Keenan, and Hector stood at the foot of the bed along with Smith, Nathaniel, and... *Frankie*. My eyes shot to my sister whose cheeks were covered in tears. She seemed uninjured save for a scratch on her brow and a small bruise below her left eye.

"Flo," I sobbed, and she ran to me, throwing her arms around my neck and crushing me with her weight. My ribs ached, but I refused to let her go. "Are you okay?"

My sister nodded as she stepped back. "I am now."

She may think that, but I could still sense the layer of hurt beyond her tired guise. I knew it was going to take a long time for us to fix what I'd done. Saving her had been the first step.

I looked at the faces around me, the men who'd risked their lives for me. I listened to them fill me in on what had happened after I thought I'd died. Hook had led the crew to shore where more of Ursa's shifters had appeared. Pascal had barely fended them off, and still managed to save Frankie.

"Once the battle was over, we waited for you to appear out of the water. The sea was so still, we started thinking the worst." Keena's voice shook. "Some of us were ready to dive in and search for you when an elderly man appeared from the sea with you clutched in his arms."

"Watch who you are calling elderly, Keenan. I may be over a hundred years old, but I won't hesitate to cut down my enemies with minimal effort." King Rylan appeared, a platter of food in his arms as my men moved to let him through.

A hundred years old?

He held out the platter. "I thought you could use something to eat."

My stomach let out a thunderous rumble that had the room doubling over with laughter. I dug in as everyone continued talking. I'd been asleep for about a week, recovering in Atlantis's infirmary. I'd nearly lost my life when the trident had been overloaded with magic. Rylan explained that the only reason I'd survived was because the goddess herself had blessed me, whatever the hells that meant. Though, I couldn't stop thinking about the voice I'd heard, the one who had helped me during my fight with Ursa and then again when I thought I'd never wake up.

"I should have said something before," I told Rylan. "It started when I was young, and only when I was near the sea. At first it was a faint humming sound, and as I got older it sounded more like someone singing without actual words. Then, after you opened up the mermaid part of me, it turned into an actual voice. One that guided me. I've always felt so connected to the sea, like she'd protected me and helped me when I needed it. I just never expected it to actually speak to me."

"What you heard wasn't exactly the sea itself, but Kai, the *goddess* of the sea. She must see something in you if she helped you defeat Ursa, which I might add was incredibly brave of you." Tears filled his eyes. "I've never been prouder."

I smiled and blinked back my own while I shoved all worries aside and instead enjoyed the company in the room. There would be plenty of time to think about Kai and why she was helping me later.

My crew dispersed, leaving King Rylan and I to speak in private.

"You have a really good group of friends, Arie." He sat down next to me, his hands resting in his lap as he smiled down at me. "I'm glad you have people who care about you. I was hoping when all this was done that you'd want to stay here. To eventually take your place as Atlantis's queen, but so much has already been taken from you. The last thing I want is to hold you back or keep you where you don't want to be."

As much as I wanted to tell him I'd love to stay, it would only be a lie. I wasn't meant for a throne, or to be tied to one place.

My life belonged to the sea and to *Black Betty*, to the vast places I still had to see with her as my steed. Rylan had done what he needed to do to keep me safe, and he'd given me a life with two amazing fathers who not only loved me and my sister but loved one another as well. I was given the gift of more than one family. I sailed the seas and went on grand adventures. There was not a single thing I would have taken back from my life…

All except that night when Malakai and Viktor were taken from me. I would never be happy here and neither would Frankie. She was what mattered to me now—her and finding out the truth about our fathers' killer.

"I can't lead an entire city when my mission is far from over. I set out all those years ago to find the one responsible for Malakai and Viktor's death. I can't stop now. I refuse to."

Frankie, who stood close enough to eavesdrop, strode up beside me with determination written on her face. "We will find answers together. Our differences aside, Arie, we will find out what happened to our fathers."

Rylan tried to hide the wince he'd given when Frankie had called them our fathers. I couldn't imagine the amount of anguish he felt in having to give away his child. Sadness cleared from his face as he looked at my sister. "I hope you do. I'll let the two of you catch up. Maybe when all of this is done the two of you can come have dinner with me in my home."

I nodded and watched as he slipped out of the infirmary. He may have been a mystery to me, a blood father I never knew I had, but I was unbelievably grateful to have met him.

"I'm glad you got to figure out the truth, Ar."

"Frankie, I—"

She held up her hand. "There's a lot we need to discuss, and I'm still pissed at you for what you did. It's going to take time for me to get over all of this, but I will. You risked your life for me and the guys filled me in on a few other things. But know this, if you ever try to leave me behind again, I'll steal Slayer and use it on you." Frankie winked before leaving to stand next to Clayton, a smile covering her face as she leaned into him.

He looked so much like his brother. From the dark hair to the blue eyes, it was like the two of them were made from the same mold. His blue shirt and breeches didn't cling to his muscles like Hook's did, but there was no denying his strong stature. The way he smiled at Frankie, the warmth between them, was a breath of relief. All I ever wanted for Frankie was for her to be happy and I hoped he'd give her that much.

"I don't think that's a sight I can get used to." Hook laughed as he took Frankie's place at my side. My heart skipped a beat as I glanced up at him. He was smiling. That faint dimple I'd seen before peeked on his cheek and it took everything in me to not comment on it. He looked truly happy for the first time since joining me on this mission.

"No, definitely not," I chuckled as I turned back just in time to see Clayton press his lips to Frankie's. "Unfortunately, she's going to end up breaking his heart."

"What makes you say that?"

I smirked. "The Lockwood girls aren't ones to be tied down to one man… or woman."

Hook shook his head, but I still saw a glint in his eyes. He peered down at me, his smile fading as he took in my battered frame. "I'm glad you're okay. I have to admit, I was angry that you took Pascal with you, but seeing the both of you afterwards, I knew it was the right call. I don't have magic or anything special coursing through me. I would have been burnt to a crisp by that beast. Last time, I only got away thanks to the winds blowing in my favor." He paused, his shoulders sinking. "You're smart, Arie, and I know we've been through hell, but I respect you as a captain. I don't know what's going to happen now that we've defeated Ursa, but I just wanted you to know that."

Was he saying goodbye?

It made sense. Hook was just as much of a captain as I was. We'd tolerated the other for the sake of saving our siblings, but now Ursa was gone and everyone was safe, we were bound to go our separate ways. Chest tightening, I cleared my throat and opened my mouth when something dawned on me.

"Hey, where's Pascal?" I asked.

Everyone in the infirmary stilled. Their conversations ended as they looked from me to the other side of the room. Where hundreds of cots that once held soulless bodies, now there was only me. And one other occupied bed, I now saw. Pascal. My hands balled into fists as my nails dug into my palms. Anger rolled through me as my gaze fell on the restraints that held Pascal's wrists and ankles. "Why is he tied up?"

Keenan placed a hand on my leg, sorrow filling his usually happy eyes. "Something's not right with him. He was hit with some sort of light after you killed the Leviathan. No one is really sure what it was, but he's been erratic ever since. He doesn't recognize any one and he nearly killed two of King Rylan's nurses who were trying to tend to his wounds. He wakes up every now and then, but he only asks for one person."

I narrowed my gaze on Keenan. "Who's that?"

"You."

"*Fuck*!" I cried out, covering the gash in my arm as I tried to reason with Pascal. "It's me, damnit. What are you doing?"

When Pascal had woken, I was there, ready for whatever he threw my way. I'd made the nurses remove the restraints the second I'd seen them on him. Pascal had spent too much time being tortured and I imagined he'd been restrained those times too. He was in an unfamiliar territory with faces he couldn't place.

I didn't understand why it was me he asked for. It had taken him a while to recognize me. I'd been too close and had felt his wrath when he hit me with his magic. He clutched his head, screaming incoherent nothings, and anytime someone got close, he'd tried to use his magic. Lucky for all of us, his magic was too weak and erratic to do much damage.

"Get it out," Pascal cried out as he slumped to his knees, his palms hitting his head. His wounds, which had just started to heal, were now open and bleeding. A trail of bloody footprints stretched along the floor while everyone else stood as far away from the wizard as they could get.

"Get what out, Pascal?" I took a step forward.

"Peter... Peter."

I turned toward Keenan who simply shook his head.

Who the *hells* was Peter?

Hook pushed his way through the crowd, his eyes wide and mouth agape as he approached. I cut him off, not wanting him to scare Pascal away. Though his eyes never reached mine. He stared at Pascal, blinking hard as if he were trying to focus on something. I looked between Hook and Pascal, but I saw nothing out of the ordinary. Did he know something I didn't?

I returned to Pascal. "Who is Peter?"

He spun toward me, a dazed look in his eyes below a furrowed brow. He shook his head and then nodded and then shook it once more before throwing his hands up. "Jumbled, messy."

"Shh... it's okay, let's sit down, maybe somewhere quiet where you can rest."

Keenan took a step forward to help, and Pascal cried out, "No!"

"Okay, okay, Pascal. No one else will touch you. Just take my hand and let me get you someplace safe."

His gaze trailed from the floor to my hands and stopped at my face, and his eyes lit up. "Little dove, is that you?"

"Yes, it's me. Would you like to take a walk?"

Something akin to happiness flickered in his face and he nodded. "There's something going on, I can't seem to think straight. It's like there's two of me living in my brain and I can't... can't..."

I placed a hand on Pascal's shoulder, and they relaxed under my grip.

He bowed his head toward me and burst into tears. "What's wrong with me?"

"Nothing," Hook called out from behind us, "Pascal, this Peter you speak of, do you know him? Do you know where he is?"

I shot Hook a glare, why was he drilling Pascal with ridiculous questions when he was in this state? "Back off, Hook."

"Arie, you don't understand. I need to know where Peter is. I've been looking for him for too long. If this wizard knows where he is, I need him to tell me." I'd never seen so much desperation coming from one person before. Even Clayton had come to his side, his gaze mirroring Hook's. What was I missing?

"You think he remembers someone from your past?" It hit me then. "Peter is the brother you left your home for, isn't he?"

Hook stepped closer to Pascal, tears shimmered in his eyes as he pleaded. "Pascal, please, where is Peter?"

Pascal lifted his head, his good eye opening and I gasped. His eye was no longer dark brown, but a light gold with flecks of dark embedded in the iris. He blinked hard, rubbing his eye as it shifted from dark brown to gold and back again. He looked at me, confusion written all over his face as he turned to Hook.

Tears cascaded down his pale face. He dropped to his knees and wailed. "I'm free, Ulrich, I'm free."

After hours of Pascal's restlessness, Rylan's nurses finally decided to sedate him again. I didn't understand what was going on, but apparently Hook did. He didn't leave Pascal's side and refused to tell me who Ulrich was, only that he's been dead for a long time.

I decided to let the two of them have their moment and joined Frankie as we walked to Rylan's home. We were taking him up on his offer of dinner, and I hoped he knew more about what was happening to Pascal. He kept mumbling on and on about this Peter person and no one on Hook's crew would tell me what was going on. They just kept staring at Hook and back to Pascal. Once the shock of whatever was going on wore off, I was going to demand someone tell me what the fuck was going on.

Until then, I had food to eat.

Rylan was waiting for us. He sat at the head of a grand table covered in flowers and seashells. Dozens of platters of food lay on top and I took in the aromas that wafted my way. A variety of meats, breads, and mead, so much of it that it would feed my entire crew for days. I was so caught up in the food that I hadn't even noticed all the other chairs surrounding the table were occupied. Men and women and children greeted Frankie and me as we took the last two seats next to Rylan.

"Thank you both for coming. These are just a few of the merfolk you saved. They wanted to thank you themselves as well as welcome you to their city. We also wanted to thank you for killing Ursa which broke the curse and allowed Atlantis to rise from the depths of the sea. It's a true honor to have you here. Both of you."

Atlantis wasn't underwater anymore. I hadn't even noticed on our walk over here, which meant it must be nighttime. Either that or I was still in shock over everything that had happened.

I looked around the room to find everyone staring back at me, nodding in thanks. I appreciated it, but I knew what Rylan was trying to do.

"While I appreciate the dinner, and the gratitude, I can't stay here. I'm so happy you all have your lives back, but mine belongs out there." I nodded toward the windows behind me.

Rylan placed a hand over mine. "You and Frankie are always welcome here, Arie. Take your time and maybe one day you'll change your mind. Now, let's eat."

He could spend an eternity thinking that, but I wasn't meant for a throne. I barely had the capability of manning a large crew, let alone an entire city. I didn't have the heart to tell the merfolk that I had no intentions of being their new queen, so rather than upset the mood, I ate.

An hour or two later, once I was overly full and ready for a nap, Frankie returned to the infirmary while Rylan led me to a much smaller den. A grand fireplace stretched along the wall, a fire cracked and hissed as it warmed the room. He gestured for me to sit, so I did. There hadn't been much time during dinner to talk, but now I could get out everything that was bothering me.

"Go ahead, ask your questions," Rylan said, his face toward the roaring fire. The light flickered against him and the resemblance between the two of us was uncanny. From the long slender nose to the same oval eyes. I had seen hardly any similarities between Ursa and me and for that I was grateful.

"When I fought the Leviathan… Ursa… the trident was supposed to hit her with my magic but instead it seemed to take hers. I didn't mean to do it and didn't even know I was until it was too late."

"The trident is a gift from the gods. There is much power that rests inside it, but it also has a mind of its own. Kai blessed the trident with the same magic she blessed you with. The trident simply worked as a vessel for your own desires. You didn't want to use the souls, or to siphon Ursa's magic, but you felt for the people who'd died under Ursa's wrath, whose souls were taken and used for evil. So, the trident did as you willed it to. It released all the souls Ursa had within her. Some of those were returned to their vessels while others rose to the afterlife."

"Those orbs, the one that hit Pascal, they were souls weren't they?"

Rylan nodded. "This could be why your friend is having difficulties with his memory. When a soul is given back to its vessel, usually it restores them back to how they were before it was taken. With Pascal, a man who was driven to insanity by torture, who spent years thinking he was someone else. A man without a soul, it may take him much longer to be able to decipher between the man he was and the man he is now."

I had to get back to Hook, to tell him what I knew. If what Rylan said was true, then it was very possible that the man Hook was looking for all these years was, in fact, Pascal. No, *Peter*.

"Though, from what the others tell me, he saved you a time or two, aiding you in your journey. A person such as Pascal wouldn't do that without a soul. It's very possible that he's linked to you in a different way. Magic is unlimited, it is in everything we touch and even in the air we breathe. Some are more linked to it than others, of course, but there's no telling what kind of effect you had on him."

Was that why he had been so drawn to me, why I was the only one who could get through to him? Pascal had come aboard my ship as one person and slowly turned into someone else entirely. The evil, terrifying wizard was now considered one of mine, a member of my crew.

"What about the Leviathan?" I asked, wanting to hold off on any more thoughts of Pascal. Not until I could talk to him some more.

"The Leviathan was a product of Ursa's dark magic. There won't be another like it and even if there was, we'd take care of it."

I sighed in relief. "When I first saw its lair on Scarlett's Lagoon and the skulls it kept, I couldn't comprehend how such a beast could do something like that, or why it would."

"That is something done by dark witches. Keeping the skulls gives them power over the dead. People can't rest until their bodies are buried, so it was a way for her to harness even more magic. Though you don't have to worry about that: once you released the souls from Ursa, they were all able to move on."

How was he so sure? Those skulls were still there and even though I released the souls from Ursa's magic, would they ever be able to cross over? Once I was done here, I'd sail to Scarlett's Lagoon and ensure every skull in that cave was put to rest. Even if it changed nothing, it was the right thing to do.

"I have one last question. Before Ursa died, she said that I may have bested her, but that I won't stop *her*. She said it as though it was about someone else. Do you know what that could have meant?"

"I don't, but I will look into it for you."

"Thank you."

Rylan and I sat there a while longer, getting to know one another a bit until the door crashed open and Keenan bolted in. Sweat dripped from his brow and he panted as he spoke. "It's Pascal."

The three of us raced to the infirmary. Inside, Pascal paced, his words frantic. "Arie," he cried out, and I stilled. I wasn't sure how to handle the fact he hadn't called me 'little dove'. "Thank the gods you're here. We need to get back to the *Betty*."

"Pascal, calm down. Tell me what's wrong?"

"It took some time, but he recognized me," said Hook. "I don't know what happened, but it's obvious she did this." The corner of his mouth curled downwards as his brows knitted together. "The torture and pain she inflicted on him made him unrecognizable. This entire time he was right here under my nose, and I didn't know."

I narrowed my eyes on him. Was he talking about Ursa? Had she done this to Pascal? She'd had his soul, from what Rylan said, but why torture him? What could she possibly gain from such a thing?

Could this be the *her* Ursa was referring to?

"I was foolish, but now I know. Now we can find the way back."

"The way back to where, Hook?"

"To Neverland."

Coming Soon:

A Land of Lost Souls
Dark and Twisted Tales Book Two

With news of where to find information about her fathers' killer, Arie travels to Neverland with a wizard who's at war with his mind, and a rival captain who battles for her heart.

Upon their arrival, they realize that the land is cursed, and its energy is dying. And at the center? A mysterious girl named Wendy and her deadly Neverbeasts. They're taking everything, leaving nothing but death and destruction in their wake. The only thing that can stop them, and cure Neverland's curse, is something that's said to have gone extinct. The same thing Arie needs to find the one who murdered her fathers.

Will Arie and her crew be able to find the light and restore Neverland? Or will the need to find her father's killer consume her instead?

Author's Note

Firstly, to my readers. I wouldn't be doing this without every single one of you who took the time to read this story. Every writing aspires to get to this point and it's here. This is my first novel and its pretty dang surreal. Thank you for your continued support and pushing me to continue Arie's story.

There's one person in my life that made this entire thing possible. If it weren't for my grandmother none of this would have happened. I was probably in 3rd or 4th grade when she started collecting all my short stories I'd write. Before long she had a whole portfolio of my work (not that it was any good at the wee age of 9). For a long time, I stopped writing and I don't really know why. It wasn't until she passed away that I decided to live up a promise I made her which was do what I loved. So here we are!

A Sea of Unfortunate Souls wasn't exactly the type of story I had in mind when I first started doing this. Urban Fantasy is my usual go to, so to write something darker and edger with a twist of fairytale was *so* much fun. I hope you enjoyed this book as much as I did writing it. I look forward to what the future holds, and I hope you will stick along for the ride.

If you enjoyed this retelling, you could also check out another retelling I did in an anthology called *Fractured Folklore*. The story I wrote is a Snow White retelling titled *The Deadliest Snow*.

If you like the Urban Fantasy setting you can also check out my short story in *Blood and Betrayal* titled *Cursed in Blood*.

Like what you've read and want to keep tabs on what's to come? You can follow me on Instagram or Facebook, you can join my Facebook group Jay R. Wolf's Pack, or you can also sign up for my newsletter!

Finally, I'd like to give a HUGE shoutout to the people who made this possible, who stuck by me through the entire process and have been pushing me to keep going.

Jared, my husband and better half who is the most amazing and supportive spouse a girl could have.

Rae, my best friend and author buddy who was my lifeline through the entire process.

Clare, my editor who went up and beyond in her duties to ensure this came out as best as it could and gave me some killer advice!

And finally… to my boys Jaxson and Luca, I do this for you my sweet boys. I love you both to the moon and beyond!

About the Author

Jay R. Wolf is an author of dark and urban fantasy, a wife and mother of three, and a huge geek.

She is from a small town in Michigan and moved to the big city to pursue her dream of acing. Though her dream of racing cars is in the wind, she finds herself in a comfy lifestyle in the Mile High city where writing fantasy has become a passion.

Her other hobbies include long walks in ancient forests where the wild things roam, gaming against evil foes, and catching fish in the great lakes.

Want to know more?
Website: www.authorjayrwolf.com
Facebook/Instagram @authorjayrwolf

www.ingramcontent.com/pod-product-compliance
Lightning Source LLC
LaVergne TN
LVHW040211200625
814264LV00028B/608